Singapore

I0635178

Allen

I was almost back to the Fairfield when someone held a gun on me. I wasn't looking around the street. I had plenty of street smarts from growing up in LA, but Singapore was basically a different world. It was exceptionally clean, and there were almost no guns here. That's why I was surprised to feel the barrel of a gun pressed to my back as I passed a dark alleyway.

"Don't make any noise, or you'll be paralyzed for life."

"What?" I couldn't believe that this was happening in Singapore.

"I said don't make any noise." The barrel dug in a little harder.

"Listen, my wallet is in my jacket pocket. Just reach in, take it, and we can both be happy, okay?" I carried a decoy wallet on me. It had a bunch of bills, but they were small bills for tipping. I used it for day to day stuff. I carried a Centurion card in my shoe;

The Reformed Bad Boy's Baby

Alyse Zaftig

ISBN: 978-1634810494

I. Present

Waking Up

it was crazy to think that I used to be awed by the Centurion cards that my clients had had in the old days. Now I was one of them, cleaned up and polished into another billionaire scion.

Mr. Flanagan had set me on the path to becoming a billionaire off of the sweat of others, and he and his friends had profited handsomely from it as well. Mr. Flanagan's shares were still under my care, except the profit would go to Trouble. There weren't many kids with 10-digit net worths; I had my own, so I didn't worry about drawing down Trouble's cash. There were accountants who kept the books, and I kept an eagle eye on it. I didn't spend much time around my son who had my dead wife Adeline's face, so I got a lot of help to deal with him. The only thing that I did was make sure that he stayed on the path to go to college. I kept a very close eye on his grades and made sure that he never slacked. The wonder of technology meant that I could look at everything that he was doing through

ParentConex, which meant that I would send over sheets of paper to be put by Trouble's bedside when he missed an assignment. He would have the academic success that Adeline would've wanted and that her parents had made a condition of his inheritance. I hoped by the time that Trouble was 30, he'd be mature enough to handle all of it on his own. Really, almost everything ran on autopilot. His maternal grandparents, the Flanagans, had been quite conservative in their investments because they were older, and I didn't move much around. Trouble would never worry about money, not with his own trust fund and my wealth. He'd never count all the cash he could find before he went to the grocery store and hope that his mother hadn't already spent it all on booze. Trouble had every material comfort that could be bought.

And if I stayed away from him, that was on me. I saw him every now and then, surprised by how much he'd grown. I lived in San Francisco half the time with a trip to Singapore every month or two. I spent very little time in Los Angeles, though my company headquarters were there, and I hired nannies and drivers to take him around when he insisted on dedicating a lot of time to swimming. I wasn't into sports growing up — just cars — so it was a mystery to me, but he had the best equipment and private lessons that money could buy.

I'd given him everything that I'd grown up without, but now all of that was in jeopardy if I didn't make it home. Unlike the Flanagans, I'd never thought about what would happen to my son if I died. He would have his college degree soon, and I was supposed to be on a flight in a few hours to make it back to LA in time to attend his college graduation.

"Hands behind your head. Move slow." The accented English meant that my mugger was a native Singaporean. I put my hands up slowly, and he reached inside of my jacket to get the decoy wallet. He opened it and saw the thick stack of bills. He grunted.

Light from headlights of a car came around, and the man tucked his gun into his waistband and went running in the opposite direction. The car kept going, and I walked the last block to my hotel.

My younger, hot-headed self would've cleaned the thief's clock before letting him take anything from me. In my neighborhood, we had a zero-sum mentality outside of the gang. Something was yours or it wasn't, and there were finite resources.

But my billionaire self said that there were things much more important than money. I should know. I had more than enough money for a lifetime. I could spend all my time surfing on the beach in LA, raising my son by myself. We'd never go hungry.

I didn't want that life. It went against everything I was to just sit and paddle a boat leisurely. I'd had a hunger in my stomach from a young age, a hunger that Adeline had bullied me into turning into success, the kind of success that came with a big house, a car, and a family.

All of that was in jeopardy if I died. I hadn't made the arrangements for Trouble to take over everything. If I died, the bank would become the trustee of Trouble's trust fund. I didn't know who inside of the bank handled that, and I needed to correct that oversight.

So I went back to my hotel, checked out, and went to the airport a few hours early. I emailed my assistant to set up some kind of meeting with my personal lawyer. I couldn't sleep tonight, not with the adrenaline from the mugging that I'd foiled still coursing through my veins. I kept muscle relaxants for the plane ride, and I knew that I'd sleep while we flew home.

Home.

Graduation

Allen

TWO DAYS LATER

I sat at a table with my son, and an awkward silence hung heavily between us. I spoke up eventually, when it was embarrassing how quiet we were.

"You're a college grad now."

Trouble looked at me and cleared his through. "Yeah, Dad, I am." Our conversation stuttered to an abrupt halt.

"You were born when I was too young, you know. Your mother and I...We had you when we were 22."

"22!" Trouble exclaimed. "I had no idea how old you were."

"I was just too young to handle a baby and a dead wife at the same time. I had my trust, of course, so I had enough money to take care of you. But all the money in the world couldn't save your mother. I threw myself into my business, although I hated the idea of making money.

What use did it have if I couldn't use it to save the woman I loved? But I'm proud of the way that you turned out, and I have Sean King to thank for that. I wasn't around much when you were younger, but that's something that I'm hoping to fix now."

I held my hand out. "Let's start fresh, okay?"

Trouble looked at me for a moment, then he shook my hand. "Okay."

"You mean it?"

"Yeah."

Then Mr. King and the rest of his family walked inside of the restaurant, and Trouble and I got to our feet as we welcomed them.

The meal was uneventful. I was quiet during it; I didn't know the King family, though I knew that Trouble had been dating Laila King for a long while. Laila's friend Nora was there, and I saw that she and Chris were carefully avoiding each other's gazes. There was a spark between the two of them.

At the end of the meal, Hudson

and Jalanda hit their wineglasses and gave graduation presents to the kids. I didn't even think about that. Trouble had everything that a kid would ever want, and if he didn't have it, he could buy it. I hadn't sent birthday presents or Christmas presents to him ever. If he expressed desire for something, it was his. I'd raised an eyebrow when I realized that some of his card charges were at a tattoo parlor and a motorcycle shop, but I'd been far more reckless as a kid. I couldn't really throw stones at his choices, not when I lived in a fragile glass house.

I was startled when Trouble got to his knee and pulled out a blue Tiffany box. He proposed to Laila. I had zero clue that he'd wanted to marry her, although I supposed that they'd been together for a while now.

After Laila said that she wanted to go to Vegas, I realized that she was dressed in a pure white dress. A bridal gown. I looked over at Jalanda King, whose eyes were moist. This whole thing had been planned, and I wasn't part of it. I just wasn't around enough for my son to keep me in the loop. After that mugging, my priorities had shifted. I already had enough money to take care of everything, and I hired the smartest people that I knew to keep my business running. I was going to start delegating more and try to take more time to get to know my son.

That's why I got into my car and headed to the Santa Monica Municipal Airport, where I could call a jet through my corporate membership with JetSuite. It was nice to fly privately, because we could dictate our takeoff time. We all ate snacks while we waited for the kids to come.

After Trouble and Laila re-joined us with their new wedding rings, we took off and landed in Vegas less than an hour later. I was slightly bemused by their quick ceremony in the Chapel of Love, but if that's what they wanted, that's what they'd get.

After the ceremony, the Kings and I said goodbye to the kids before going up to our rooms. Flying took a lot more out of me than it used to, and I was glad to see that someone had left complimentary Guinness in my suite. I'd stayed at this hotel before for a conference, and somebody had paid attention to my preferences. I made a mental note to tip the hotel staff in some way and compliment the manager.

I got out of my suit and went to bed, ignoring the emails on my phone, the red icon showing that I had more than I cared to read.

Urgent Call

Allen

The next morning, I woke up to a phone call on my cell.

I accepted the call without opening my eyes. Then I said, "What?" My voice was low since I had just woken up.

"You didn't answer my email last night, sir." The person on the other end was Ellie, my executive assistant.

"What email?" I yawned. It was

too early for this shit.

"The email telling you that you needed to give an answer about what measures we would take to repel the hostile takeover of Star."

That got my attention. I'd taken a shine to the CEO of Star, a young man who reminded me of myself a long time ago.

Star had a generous employee equity plan, too generous. The sudden success and growth of the company meant that secretaries could sell their stock and leave, using their millions to live comfortable lives.

A new VC company, Majuscule, had slowly been eating up all the stock that the former employees had sold. In the hands of dozens of employees, it wasn't a problem. But gathered together, they had enough stock to change things.

Star wasn't the first company that Christopher had founded, but it was the first time that he'd handled employees. His dad must've been allergic to money or something, because Christopher was very open-handed. A little too open-handed.

I wasn't surprised when we'd had a letter from Majuscule with some demands that picked at the way that Christopher ran the company. Because he was young, he had hired a lawyer who didn't know how to run startups. The lawyer had given voting stock to the employees instead of common stock without voting rights.

We would win, of course, but Majuscule would give us one hell of a fight while we protected the company from their insanity. They wanted to take Christopher out as the CEO and install their own. They also wanted to put in a new CFO to supervise the kid if Christopher couldn't be ousted.

None of that was happening on my watch.

"Call my lawyers," I told her. "They'll take care of this."

"I already did, sir. They copied me on the email that they sent to you."

"Give me the 60-second version, Ellie."

"We've got to have a war council

right away. The situation is delicate. It's possible to rescind some of the shares or ask the current employees to forfeit theirs before they mature, but Christopher doesn't want to punish his loyal, current employees for the sake of the ones who left."

"Makes sense." I checked the time. "I'll be back as soon as I can."

"Back? Sir, I thought that you were in Los Angeles for your son's graduation."

"I am. I was. I'm in Vegas."

"Vegas?" My assistant's tone said

that she never considered that I even did leisure activities.

"My son just got married."

She sputtered for a moment before saying, "Congratulations, Mr. McKane."

"Thank you." I picked up my clothes from yesterday. I hadn't had time to pack anything. When I brought them to my nose, I was relieved to find out that they didn't smell too bad at least.

I called the hotel concierge.

"Hello?"

"What can I do for you?"

"I need to contact Hudson and Jalanda King. I arrived here with them, but I don't know their room number."

"One moment, sir." I could hear the clack of the concierge's keyboard. "They are in Suite 295."

"Thank you."

"You're welcome, sir."

I hung up the phone, then I read the instructions on the phone for how to call other people inside of the hotel. I'd been in enough to know that every hotel had a different way of doing things. I tapped the right keys to ring their phone, and it only rang once before someone answered.

"Hello?" Hudson's voice was low, like mine.

"I'm sorry to wake you like this, but I've got to get back to LA soon."

"What's going on?"

"Hostile takeover," I told him grimly. "I've got to get back."

"We'll get packed up. Okay if we skip breakfast? Scratch that. I'll just have the catering company come to the airfield and tell them to put breakfast in your jet."

My stomach growled. I'd pass on the powdered eggs that the hotel breakfast buffet would serve.

"Sounds good to me."

"Meet you downstairs in an hour." Hudson hung up the phone.

I had nothing packed, just my wallet and keys, both of which I kept in my laptop case which had been in my car when I went to the graduation. I went to the bathroom to take a shower, rinsing off the dust

from a day's worth of traveling. The
hotel shampoo smelled like a
woman's shampoo, full of flowery
fragrance. I would smell like a chick,
but at least I'd be clean.

Leaving Vegas

Allen

An hour after I rang Hudson's phone, we were all downstairs in the lobby, except for his son, Chris.

I checked my watch. "We need to get to the airport within 30 minutes of when I told them to be ready. If I get there first, we can hold the plane."

"Chris will be here anytime now."

I felt itchy. I wasn't a patient

man, not when ruthless barbarians were knocking on my door.

"Look, I'll take a taxi out there first, okay? I'll meet you there."

Jalanda and Hudson exchanged a look before simultaneously telling me, "Okay."

My heart ached at the quiet communication that showed that they were a team. I'd had about a year with my wife before she was gone. Hudson probably took it for granted, but he was one lucky bastard. He had a wife and two kids who loved them both. I had a son that I barely knew. I'd promised Trouble that I'd make an effort, and I would, after he was done with his honeymoon in Vegas.

I went up to the front desk to ask for one of their cars, and I was on my way within two minutes. I tipped the driver 20% on top of the exorbitant hotel charge, and I got into the jet. I pulled out my laptop and began going through the deluge of email associated with the hostile takeover.

When Chris, Hudson, and

Jalanda came into the plane, I acknowledged them. With everybody aboard, the pilot did the pre-flight check. Strapped in, I counted the seats. There were small plates with croques monsieurs on them and Saran wrap on top that was steaming up from the heat of the sandwiches. I ate mine.

There were seven seats on this plane, although one of them was a small couch. Every seat had been taken on the way out. There were four sandwiches, though. Were we missing somebody?

I thought back to yesterday's dinner. There was a dark-skinned girl, Nora, I think, who wasn't on the plane with us. Maybe she was coming back with Trouble and Laila.

In any case, it wasn't my problem. I had much more urgent matters to deal with, so I went back and read through everything that the lawyers had sent me.

It looked like we'd have enough pull to handle it, so long as we yanked the non-vested voting shares from the current employees.

Christopher wasn't going to like it,

but we had to do it or lose control of

the company entirely. It was going to

be a hard sell, for sure, but high-

pressure, high-stress situations like

this were the ones that had made my

career.

I put together notes in a file

about the different avenues that I

thought that we could take to achieve

our objectives.

The flight back to Los Angeles felt

fast, probably because I was buried

in my laptop the whole time.

When we began our descent into Santa Monica Municipal Airport, I finally closed my laptop and put it in my lap.

"Man, Trouble was right."

I turned to look at Chris, who was across the aisle. He'd played video games or something during the flight.

"What?"

"You work all the time. You're a workaholic."

I bristled under the accusation.

"I am not a workaholic. I just have things to do. I'm sure your father does that, too."

"Yeah, but he doesn't do it during family time. Look at him and my mom."

Jalanda was asleep on Hudson's shoulder, and I had to suppress a pang of envy.

"I'm working on it," I said stiffly before turning away from Chris and looking out my window as we came closer to the ground. I didn't know Chris very well, though he and

Trouble had gotten into a fair number of messes together. Chris was a fighter, and he loved to drag Trouble into it. My boy seemed to have the cooler head of the two, from what their teachers and coaches had said, but Trouble ended up with bloody knuckles just as often as Chris did. Though the Kings were horrified, I was proud that my boy could take care of himself, especially after taking martial arts classes...maybe jiu jitsu? I hadn't paid attention; I just made sure that his bills were always paid.

He had carte blanche and more money than he could spend in a lifetime, so we didn't worry about our daily expenses.

When the plane touched down, the slight bump woke up Jalanda. She rubbed her eyes and reached for Hudson's hand. I had to admit that I envied the casual intimacy. I hadn't ever lacked for female companionship, but a wife was something more than an easy, no-strings arrangement. There'd been a few women who'd wanted more —

money makes you a thousand times more handsome — but I'd sent them away, one after another.

Adeline held a special place in my heart, a place that nobody else in the world could touch. My heart had healed with a gigantic scar, and I was almost surprised that it didn't show on the outside.

Then the pilot was telling us that we could take off our seat belts, so I took off mine and picked up my laptop case, shoving my laptop inside of it.

"Thanks for coming," I told the King family.

"Thank you for paying for the charter. I can reimburse you."

I waved my hand. "It's fine." The money that it cost was less than the interest that I earned in a day.

"Our kids are married now, so I guess that we're family."

I blinked. I guessed that it was true. "Okay. Family." I hadn't had a real one in a long time.

Jalanda suddenly hugged me, and I reached down a second later to hug her. I didn't get spontaneous, friendly hugs. Ever. Hudson slapped me on the back. Chris was a little more wary, probably because he thought that I was some distant ogre that only yelled at Trouble when he got bad grades.

"Bye," I told them. They waved at me as I walked back to the car that I'd parked when we left to go to Vegas the day before.

When I got back into my car and started it, I breathed a sigh of relief. I wasn't used to having to deal with people. When a woman went to sleep in my bed, I made sure that I was out of it before she was awake. I would have the closest diner bring out pancakes for breakfast every time, so I was sure that the end of her stay was good. But my housekeeper in San Francisco would gently shoo away anybody who wanted to wait for me. She knew the drill, even if she didn't approve. She had five kids of her own, and she'd made her opinion of my parenting quite clear.

Frankly, so had the Ecuadorian

housekeeper that I kept in Los Angeles. Though Trouble's nannies had come and gone, as had his drivers, the housekeeper stayed the same. She knew the way that I liked the house, and it was a lot harder to find someone who would put up with my quirks than to find replacement nannies. She was something of a mother figure to Trouble.

Still thinking about Trouble, I drove to the office, still dressed in yesterday's clothes.

War Council

Allen

When I walked into the main conference room, everyone turned to look at me. They stared.

"What?"

I touched the corner of my mouth, but there wasn't any food there.

"Get lucky last night?" my lawyer said, smirking.

"Excuse me?"

"Your clothes look like you've rolled around in them."

I looked down. There were more creases than usual in my shirt. I hadn't bothered to hang it up yesterday.

"I was in Vegas."

"That's what Ellie said, but I didn't believe her. What, did you go on a bender last night?"

I shrugged. "No. My son got married."

My lawyers stared at me with their mouths open. "I didn't know you had a son." I used different lawyers for my personal and corporate matters, and I remembered that I had wanted to rearrange things after the mugging in Singapore, which seemed like a lifetime ago. My son's marriage had turned everything upside down, and I was waiting for my assistant to schedule something for me.

"I do." I pulled out my laptop. "Enough talk. Let's get down to business."

Majuscule had issued a long list of demands which were frankly absurd and totally crazy. We read through them, figuring out which ones were the least objectionable. The meeting went late into the night, so long that we ordered two meals during it, and when I looked up again, it was suddenly nighttime.

I yawned.

"Okay, team. Let's pack it up. We'll reconvene at 7 tomorrow morning."

We packed up the delicious but fattening Chinese food that we had ordered to keep ourselves going and put it all away.

I went home, then. Trouble was still in Vegas, so I had the house to myself.

When I thought about it, I realized that I hadn't spent much time on my own in a long time. I'd never had a problem getting female company. During the day, I wore bespoke suits that fit better than any Zegna suit ever could. In bed, the ladies seemed to like my gang tattoos. They said that it made me dangerous. I'd considered laser surgery, since I could definitely afford it, but I didn't want to. The tattoos told a story that I didn't often tell.

It occurred to me that I might want to call my son more often, but probably not while he was on his honeymoon. I decided to set up some father-son bonding time. I hadn't ever taken my boy to a ball game. He was a swimmer, and I wasn't an athlete. Trouble had a motorcycle, which I paid for through his trust fund, but it had been a long time since I'd been on a motorcycle.

What was it about getting older that made you crave fewer dangerous things? As a young man, even with Adeline's influence, I'd liked to live on the edge, rock climbing, parasailing, zip-lining, and all the extreme sports that I could find. But after her death, I had sunk into a funk. I couldn't bear to do all the things that I used to do with her anymore. It killed me to think that I'd spent so long basically underwater.

I'd built a big business, but I didn't need it. My investments would keep me afloat for life. I should probably buy an expensive yacht to burn through my money at this point or set up a huge charitable foundation. Trouble, when I was dead, would be a billionaire several times over. There was no point in having that much money. I had seen the sons of my business associates lead lives of debauchery and nonsense, which was the key reason why Trouble didn't know quite how much he had. He just knew that he had a certain allowance and that all of his daily living expenses, including cars, motorcycles, or other transportation, would always be covered. I could've had a family of a dozen children with Adeline, and none of them would have ever needed anything.

I put a hand over my chest. Adeline existed in a corner of my heart that I seldom visited anymore. It was too painful to think of the love of my life and the path that we'd not taken together. She'd been stolen from me far too young, and I needed her.

But the pain of her loss was an old scar now, though it still hurt. I needed to focus on connecting with the family that I still had, my son.

So instead of asking my assistant to handle things at this late hour, I clicked around on the Dodgers site. I frowned. I couldn't easily see an option for getting a box.

I took out my phone and sent a quick email to my assistant asking her to take care of it. It had taken me a long time to find Ellie, but she was a perfect fit. She had been an executive assistant for more than a decade, and she was extremely competent. She loved working for me because I only asked things of her during normal working hours, and those hours for her were seven to three so that she could spend time with her kids. I didn't care when she did the work, as long as it got done.

What were good father-son bonding activities? I felt like a ball game would be a good choice, but I was woefully inept when it came to choosing anything else. My father was gone when I was a child. I remembered trips to the zoo and aquarium once in a while, but I believed that Trouble was a little old to take to the zoo and take pictures of orangutans.

We would start with a ball game then. I had no idea of what he liked. We could go to swimming competitions, I supposed, but Trouble didn't swim competitively at USC. He just stopped when he had gone to college, and he only swam recreationally these days. Maybe a water polo game would be good.

I sighed and ran my hands through my hair. It was harder to be a good father than a negligent one, that was for sure.

I went downstairs to our home gym to run off some of the frustration. A good amount of cardio could always fix me after a long day like today.

As I ran, I heard the pounding rhythm in my head as I thought about our next steps. I never ran with music on, because it interfered with my thoughts. The thumps of my feet hitting the treadmill and the squeal of the treadmill as it ran were the only accompaniment. I considered running moving meditation. It had served me well, always helping me focus on whatever I needed to figure out.

By the time that an hour had passed, my back was soaked with sweat and I was dripping sweat onto the front of the treadmill. I knew that it was time to stop when my legs started feeling like jelly.

It had been a long time since I had substantially pushed myself in any way. I had been living life on a totally even keel. Where was the young gang leader who had made a fortune hustling on the streets? I felt like I had lost my younger self, too, when my wife had died and my hopes for the future were utterly shattered.

I slowly walked up the stairs, using the handrail for support. I wasn't a young man anymore. I wasn't out of shape, but I certainly wasn't able to keep up the same kinds of speeds that I used to run at.

I turned on the shower. Even through Los Angeles had an extreme drought, I had to admit that I used more water than was strictly necessary. The cost of the water was negligible for me, and Trouble and I had a much smaller household than one packed with the dozen kids that Adeline and I had never had.

When I was done, the mirror was fogged over. I dried off and wrapped a towel around my waist. I put on boxers before I went into my empty bed, then I stared at the ceiling while I thought about what tomorrow would bring. I figured that Trouble and Laila would come back to Los Angeles, so I'd send another email to my assistant to schedule a box for a game after he came back.

I chased my thoughts around and around my head until I finally fell into an exhausted sleep.

Plans

Allen

The next day, I woke up feeling more rested than I had ever been. I hadn't realized it before today, but it felt like there was a monkey riding on my back that had been there forever. Now that I was finally making strides to take care of my family, it felt like it had evaporated. Though my legs were sore from yesterday's run, I knew that I felt better than I had in a long time.

I went into work to do the same thing that I'd done yesterday. We had several different plans of attack. I hired the best and the brightest; I especially looked for good negotiators, who were key on any team. I tested them with their salary negotiations. I had to admit that I certainly enjoyed sparring with them, and the skills of my lawyers meant that I got a bigger piece of the pay than I'd be able to get myself.

Soon, we were done for the day.

The lawyers packed up their briefcases and went back to their office.

Ellie was waiting for me when I was done.

"When do you want the tickets for, sir? We have a game coming up tomorrow and another one a week from then."

"A week from then, please, Ellie." I nodded at her. I trusted her totally, and I could always expect her to finish what she was given very promptly.

"Of course, sir." She went back to her desk. A year ago, she had told me that working for me was easier than working for other executives. Using their names always made people jump, of course, but using my name made them jump a little higher. Though I was demanding of my employees, setting a very high bar, I was always a very generous employer. They had good Christmas boni, and Ellie's car had been paid for with one. Ellie knew that our relationship was a symbiotic one; she made my life easier, and I made hers easier, too. She was a single mom; all of her time was eaten up by raising her kids. They were cute, and I paid for their private school education at one of the local Jesuit schools where I used to sell.

It's funny how small the world is. I used to deal at all the school where I'd sent Trouble, and I knew the locations of all the private schools in Los Angeles that had existed twenty years ago.

I hoped that my son hadn't used,

but I supposed that it would have a detrimental impact on his swimming. He was a competitor, a shark, and I didn't believe that Trouble would handicap himself like that. But I didn't know how I would ever start asking him what his preferences were.

It wasn't like I had a high hill to stand upon. I'd dealt the stuff, though I'd never used it. I saw first-hand how addiction changed people's lives and put them at the mercy of their dealers. It was good to be a dealer, and it was bad to be on the other side. Adeline's parents had forced her to cross to the side of the angels, and I'd always be grateful for that. I loved her deeply, and I knew that Adeline's enforced rehab was a better choice than any other one on the path that she had ended up going down.

I had to admit, though, that losing all of my friends, the members of my gang, had been a hard pill to swallow. Gino had been locked up for a long time. When that car heist had gone wrong, he'd ended up killing the someone. He didn't get a life sentence because he was a minor, but he'd be in jail for around 25 years, maybe with a little parole.

I blinked as I realized that it was somewhere around 25 years from the first time that I had taken the reins of the gang before I relinquished them at Adeline's request. I'd had a small amount of power on the street before I'd given all of it away. I didn't know anything about moving drugs, although I had noticed when

California nearly decriminalized marijuana due to their overflowing jails.

Gino was probably out now, I realized as I thought about the whole thing more. California had pushed a lot of people out on parole when it was obvious that the jails couldn't handle the people who were in there now. They were at triple capacity with more arriving each day, and the state budget didn't really have more money for them. The government of California was nearly bankrupt at times, and it certainly didn't help that Los Angeles was a major port of activity for several different criminal elements. I'd been one in the ancient past.

I rubbed my calf, which was spasming. I was too old to run around the streets, looking over my shoulder for cops, learning the alleyways so that I could slip into the shadows at a moment's notice. It turned out that legitimate business was both far more lucrative and easier; I could get bank accounts, for one thing. Sure, I paid taxes now like a good citizen, but my taxes were a small price to pay for the protection of the justice system rather than its pursuit. I had accountants who could make numbers dance, so we had plenty of offshore accounts in the Bahamas. I believed in paying what I owed. In college I'd learned from my accounting professors on the very first day of Accounting 101 that tax avoidance was a crime while tax minimization was not. Everybody paid the least that he could, which was how the system worked. The IRS only came after the people who paid less than they should. To be honest, the IRS was woefully underpowered and underfunded. Nobody liked the idea of giving the IRS more power, so they did their job as best they could, auditing when they could.

After my stomach grumbled, I ordered food from a Thai place that was only five minutes away from my house. It was a tiny place that was mostly a hub for delivery with a kitchen; real estate in this part of Los

Angeles cost an absolute fortune, but they did brisk business. Thai food was good in two respects: one, it was tasty and healthy, and two, it was quick to prepare. I didn't have Adeline to remind me to eat my vegetables, but I tried to get some when I could. My housekeeper kept food stocked in the kitchen, and I could've had carrots anytime that I wanted. But I was too lazy to go down to the fridge and get food out to cook; I wasn't a good cook anyway, which was why I had a housekeeper in the first place. If I gave her advance notice, she would take care of any meals that I wanted her to make. I ate out more often than I ate in, and I was rarely in Los Angeles, but over the years, she had learned about my likes and dislikes as well as my minor allergies. The thought came to me then that I should probably give her a raise. I gave her a ten percent one every year, but she probably deserved more for having been a surrogate mother to Trouble while he was essentially abandoned on the beach.

I was suddenly stunned to realize that I hadn't been to the beach in over two decades. Adeline and I used to go frequently since she loved the ocean, and it had broken my heart to try to go after she was dead. But if I wanted to heal the gaping wound that still existed in the center of my chest, I should keep on doing the things that reminded me of my beautiful dead wife.

Swimming Trunks

Allen

So I went upstairs to change into my swimming trunks. They were ancient, older than Trouble, in fact. They were in good condition in a drawer, though they were pushed to the very bottom. I smelled them, and they smelled okay. My housekeeper must put something in my drawers to keep away insects and it had a little bit of a citrus scent.

I put my shorts on and looked at how they fit. Even though I'd worked hard in the last 20 years, I still could fit into my trunks. I touched my stomach. A long time ago, when I cared, I'd kept a six-pack. It was easy when I was a teenager. I still had the upper two abdominal muscles, but the rest were lost under a basically straight sheet. I wasn't fat, but I wasn't ripped, either.

The reason being that I had an office job which entailed sitting on my butt all day. I made a note to start doing more core work and strength training. My body had atrophied from the shape that I'd kept it in earlier, when it had mattered for Adeline, and I knew that I hadn't cared enough about any of my partners since she died to maintain my body in the same kind of shape. I'd also had a distinct shortage of time once I entered the venture capital business, because I was always on. I sometimes hired a temp to be a backup for Ellie; though she was competent, I sometimes needed somebody in the afternoon.

The temp service sent a wide variety of temps, some of whom were competent and others who were not. The competent ones tended to find permanent, full-time positions elsewhere while the others kept on drifting through. I had a weird policy that my HR team didn't like; I always provided health insurance for my temps while they were around. We'd worked out something with Kaiser. It was common knowledge that we did it, and people jumped over themselves to apply for any job postings that we put up on our website. For any given position, we would have to wade through a few hundred resumes to find the dozen or so that we would call for an in-person interview for the temp position.

I walked down to get into my car. I'd bought a Tesla Roadster back when Tesla was shiny and new, and it still ran like a dream. I'd get a Model X at some point, when I cared enough to buy one. Right now, the waiting time was so long that I could buy a new car now and drive it for a year before they delivered my Model X. I wasn't the kind of guy who liked to wait for my cars, and the Roadster was a sports car that handled easily. The maintenance was easy, too, since the electric motor was the only part that needed to be taken care of. Ellie didn't schedule oil changes or anything; twice a year, she would drive my car over to the Pep Boys closest to my house so that they could take a look and balance my tires.

I turned my car on, and it

chirped at me. I headed straight for Redondo Beach. Manhattan Beach had too many memories for me.

When I got there, I saw a huge parking structure. It hadn't been there the last time that I had gone to Redondo, and I realized that Los Angeles had grown without me while I'd stayed stuck in my grief and sadness, the pain numbed by throwing myself into my work. It felt like I was Rip van Winkle coming out of the cave after a long time spent in the dark. The lot was big enough that

I could easily find a parking space. I went to one of the machines to pay for the slot that I had taken. I liked the system there, and the parking space wasn't too expensive. I swiped a card, since I didn't keep much change on me.

Soon, I was at the boardwalk and taking in the smells. There was a lot of seafood, of course, but I could smell the fried scent of french fries and funnel cakes. Adeline always tried to keep me out of the ice cream parlors near the beach, but I'd always pulled her in. No matter how often she protested that ice cream was fattening, I knew that it was secretly one of her favorite foods.

I wondered what Trouble's favorite ice cream flavor was. I rubbed at the center of my chest as I realized that I had no clue what his preferences were. My adult son, now a college graduate and soon to be trust fund kid, wasn't a child anymore.

He'd been given a better childhood than my own, but he'd

basically grown up without a father, too.

I wanted things to be different, but I guessed that he'd be moving out so that his young bride could have some privacy. I couldn't blame him. Adeline may have waited for after the wedding, but we had a no-clothes policy at home unless we had guests over...and we rarely did, choosing to entertain in restaurants, clubs, and bars.

After I smelled a delicious scent, I went and ate a funnel cake with powdered sugar on the top. Yes, it was totally fattening and terrible for me, but it was also fun. I hadn't had much of a childhood, learning to cope by myself at a very early age. And now that I'd missed my son's childhood, it seemed that I wouldn't have much of an opportunity.

Trouble would have a kid someday. I rubbed the back of my neck when I thought about being a grandfather in the next few years. I was still young, two decades away from retirement, and it seemed insane to me that my son would have

a baby so soon. He was married,

though. I didn't know much about

Trouble and Laila, but I did see the

way that he looked at her. I guessed

that they'd have a kid within the next

two years.

I smiled. It might be nice to have

a baby around, though I didn't know

much about them. Mrs. Flanagan

had always kept a watchful eye on me

when I played with Trouble. I'd

wanted to wrestle with him when he

tackled me when he was still

unsteady on his feet, but Mrs.

Flanagan said that roughhousing was

strictly forbidden in her house. She'd

raised a daughter, Adeline, and

Adeline wasn't the kind of girl that

got mud on her shoes while she

played. To be honest, she was

fastidious, checking all of her clothes

for tears and loose threads before

wearing them. When the laundry

service took care of our clothes, she

would discard them the instant that

one had a loose thread. It was good

enough for me, but it was never good

enough for her. I guessed that when you grew up with as much money as the Flanagans had, you could afford to throw away any clothing that you liked, but I always thought you could save a little money with a tiny bit of needle and thread.

I got to the end of the boardwalk and sat down on a bench. There were a lot of people here fishing, and the sea was beautiful and turbulent. There were little kids climbing the rails, which seemed like a safety hazard to me. Their parents didn't seem to care though. When I spent more time watching, I realized that they moved with practiced grace up and around the rails. They must do it often. This area was their playground and the rails were their equivalent of a jungle gym.

I sat there, watching the hustle and bustle of people coming in and out of the boardwalk, until there were very few people left anymore and the wind made the air too chilly for me to sit there anymore. I walked back to my car and drove home.

Mutiny

Allen

I'd left my phone at home, not wanting to be disturbed. As soon as I walked into the house, it started to ring. I lunged for it, because Ellie's name was on the front. I put it on speaker.

"Hello?"

"Sir...I need you to come into the office right away." Ellie didn't work at night, so I knew that it was an emergency just because she was talking to me now.

"Majuscule just sent a letter to the board of directors, and we're looking at serious mutiny inside of the company. Because Star's employees have realized that they have the deciding votes here, they've decided to ask for higher salaries."

"I'll be right there." We still hadn't succeeded in convincing Christopher to yank the voting shares away from the employees whose stock hadn't yet vested, but our backs were against the wall. It was time to do it, whether the CEO approved or not.

I was the chairman of the board, but Christopher had brought on a lot of experienced people from different sectors. They all had a substantial amount of common stock, so they didn't have the right to vote. However, Christopher still answered to them, and if they decided that his leadership wasn't the best thing for the company, he'd find himself on the other side of the door.

That was the life of a startup

founder. With the traction that Star had, a major player in the mobile payment processing space, Christopher's departure would not mean the death of the company. The board of directors would look for a replacement, somebody who could run the company in his place. Majuscule had somebody in mind, but I was damned if I was going to let them put some puppet in charge of Star.

I drove into work, and the whole gang was there. Some of them had changed, while others hadn't. I looked down and realized that I was in my boardwalk clothes, swimming trunks and a faded t-shirt.

"What are we doing?" I demanded of the war council. "What steps will we take?"

"We'll just do Plan C, sir. We wanted to take the hostile part out of this takeover, but we'll choose the Pac-Man defense."

I nodded. Sometimes, when a company was small enough, we could talk to the bank into fronting us a business loan to acquire them. I wondered how it would feel inside of Majuscule when my own company turned around and did the exact same thing to them. They would scurry like rats on a sinking ship. They would be sorry that they had ever messed with Star.

I smiled, and the lawyers around me stared. I knew that the swimming trunks and t-shirt were a far cry from my usual attire, but it did them good to be pushed off-balance once in a while.

"Let's go."

They nodded as all of us opened our laptops to work on the plan. I would set up a meeting with my banker, with whom I played golf once a month, to talk about getting the capital for this play. We had cash, sure, and we had over a billion dollars in stock. But the quantity of cash that we had on hand was limited. We normally plunged it into investing in business, and a lot of our stock was locked up in our companies. We'd be able to offer some collateral, but the bank was necessary for the cash that we needed today. It would make things run a little close to the edge, but we'd tighten our belts until we saw this through.

Ellie was in the corner, taking notes of everything that was going on. When I got to my feet, she came to my side.

"Sir?"

"Ellie, I want you to set up a meeting with my banker for lunch tomorrow. Take him to that place he likes." Il Segreto wasn't really a secret, but it had a delicious name. My banker was partial to their saltimbocca, which I had to admit was one of the best things that I'd ever tasted. It was pricy, though, and my banker loved to be wined and dined. I admitted that I wouldn't say no to a little wine, good food, and good company in the middle of the work day.

I waved goodbye to the lawyers as they pieced together the documents for the takeover. Some of them were better versed in repelling hostile takeovers rather than implementing them, but all of my lawyers were quick on their feet. I only kept the best and the brightest around me, and I paid them well exactly for moments like this. I didn't keep in-house counsel, but I'd used one firm from the early days. I was one of their biggest clients, and without me, the firm wouldn't have grown to the size that it was now. It was a symbiotic relationship, because if they threw me to the curb, I would have no idea where to start. They knew where the skeletons were buried.

Without my business, they would have to lay off a quarter of their staff. Maybe even a third. They relied on the substantial amount of work that I generated for them, and I helped with their recruiting process. A lot of their young associates were green, and they were put through simple requests from me to prove their mettle. It was both high-pressure and low-profile, and that suited me just fine. Older lawyers would look through their work, and I knew that they only hired from the top 10% of each law class. There were too many lawyers in LA, but finding the good ones was the hardest trick. Separating the wheat from the chaff was a task in itself, meaning that two of the lawyers of my law firm were full-time recruiters given the size of the company.

I drove home again, this time going straight upstairs and falling asleep. The excitement of the day, my run, my trip to the boardwalk and memory lane, and the counterstrike that we had planned got to me, and I slept soundly while still dressed in my swimming trunks and t-shirt.

Sweat

Allen

When I woke up, I could see the cold light of dawn outside of my window. It was a smoggy day, so I couldn't see the sun, but it was still there behind the clouds of gray. I showered and peeled off my clothing. There was sweat all over my lower body, and it wasn't from any kind of fun activities. I went to the shower and washed myself off, though I'd showered the day before. I refused to feel guilt about the waste of water.

When I got to work, a ton of documents were sitting on my desk. I took the time to read through all of them carefully, but I knew that they would be right. They contained everything that we needed to do.

I sat and waited for the clock to tick down to my lunch meeting with James, my banker.

We met at Il Segreto, and, like always, we both ordered the saltimbocca and a little white wine.

When the server took our menus away, we got down to business.

"So what's this all about? The last time that you knocked on my door, you were trying to acquire a little startup. What was it?"

"It was Star."

"Yeah. The valuation was crazy for a team that only had a dozen people on it."

I shrugged. "Those were a dozen engineers. If Instagram could sell to Facebook for a billion dollars with only 33 employees, it wasn't unreasonable to value Star where it was. In America, wireless technology might be in its infancy, but it's coming. How many places do you go without your phone?"

"Not many."

"Exactly. Imagine being able to tip your waiter directly, not give them a card to swipe and get a receipt to sign. Imagine being able to pay your subway fare with your phone, which is normal in Japan. There are many things that we can unlock with phones. Do you know that people who use their mobile phones to shop don't comparison shop?"

"So they aren't coupon clippers...they'll just buy whatever they see at the price that they're given."

"Normally, mobile shoppers are on the go or not inclined to actually do research. There's an absolute fortune to be made in handling mobile commerce, and believe me, we're on the forefront of it. Christopher's team is a bunch of the smartest people you've ever met."

"And now what company do you want to acquire?"

I sighed. "We have to buy out another VC firm."

His eyes bugged out. "What?"

"They are trying to take control of Star because they see the potential of it. They want their own man to take the helm, and they don't understand that Christopher is the one who makes the magic happen."

"Well, how much money are we talking about?"

I named a number. He swallowed

hard.

"Allen, look. I came to this lunch meeting with you because I'm authorized to hand out business loans to people who can afford to pay them back. But the number that you just said is way beyond my pay grade."

I looked at him. "10 percent annual interest."

He slumped in his chair. "Holy shit."

"Do you want it? Because if you don't, I'll just..."

He held up a hand. "Don't talk. I have to think."

He stared at the ceiling. I watched as his lips moved silently and his fingers flicked. He sighed.

"We can do it."

I didn't smile, but I wanted to. I didn't want him to know that there were no other options. Ellie had taken a quick peek at other banks, but none of them would back me in a venture this big. It had been James or no one, and the saltimbocca and two glasses of wine had done the trick.

There was a philanthropy study that showed that people were most generous when they had two drinks. People who were sober were tight-fisted. People who were drunk were aware that their judgment was impaired, so they didn't sign checks. Charities kept enough wine in your system to feel good but not enough to feel drunk so that they could maximize donations. That's why all the fundraisers had two drink tickets for every attendee.

And those two drinks had put together the final piece in my strategy to take over Majuscule and metaphorically display their heads on my wall.

"That interest is going to compound monthly, okay?"

I spread my hands. "Whatever makes you happy, James."

He blew out a long breath. "If I didn't know you, you asshole, I'd never agree to this. My ass is on the line for this. If you don't pay it back…"

I put my fist on the table, and he jumped as the silverware clattered on the floor.

"It'll be paid." No matter what it took, this crazy gamble would pay off, or I'd know why. My own company was on the line here. I'd come out to protect Star like a mother wolf protecting her little puppy. Star was my key to eleven figures, and nobody was going to take that away from me.

It turned out that even outside of the neighborhood where I'd grown up, I'd kept my zero-sum mentality. I kept what was mine, and I would follow through on the promise of Star and see it rise.

James was shaking his head. "I'll have our lawyers draft something up and send it to yours."

I held out my hand for him to shake. "Thank you."

He just shook his head and didn't shake mine. "I hope you know what you're doing, Allen."

"I do."

I threw a few hundred in cash on the table before James and I stood up to go to the door. I was filled with elation that I'd clinched a major milestone on my way to making the Majuscule people regret the day that they decided to usurp my company. Just as they had, we would send information to their board of directors and watch them scurry like ants when their jobs were in jeopardy.

Ball Game

Allen

The takeover of Majuscule was going on full blast when Trouble and Laila finally called my customer happiness representative and asked for a jet to bring them home from Vegas. It was one day before the ball game, and I texted Trouble.

Want to go to a Dodgers ball game?

His text in reply was brief.

Yeah. But Laila hates sports.

I smiled.

Just you and me, then.

Yup.

I wondered if our time together was going to be as awkward as the time that we'd spent together at his graduation dinner, but I put that to the side. I had shirked my duty to my son long enough, and we'd wade through all the years of silence and virtual abandonment until we learned more about one another.

* * *

The next afternoon, I played hooky from work for a little bit. I left after lunch to go to the game, and it felt good to be out in the mid-day Los Angeles sunshine, not a care in the world besides spending time with my boy.

He met me at the stadium, and he was surprised when I led him to the boxes.

"You paid for a box?"

"Yes." Was that strange? Both of us were billionaires, even if Trouble had no idea of the actual extent of his wealth.

"I didn't know how that worked. I wondered if they only went to season ticket holders."

"They do. Ours only goes to season ticket holders."

"How did you get that? The list is a decade long."

I shrugged. "Money talks." I didn't know the details, but Ellie had carte blanche to draw on my personal account for a certain amount. That amount was fairly high; I reviewed all of her decisions at the end of the month, but she'd never messed up.

She knew what she was doing, and I

had total faith in her, enough to pay

her for three months of maternity

leave for each kid. She was

irreplaceable.

We went up to our box.

Inside, there was an assortment

of food. I guessed that they had some

kind of catering company taking care

of everything, because there were

sandwiches. The bread wasn't the

cheap white stuff that fell apart in

your hands, either. No, these were

kaiser rolls and potato rolls that were delicious. With the freshly carved roast beef and turkey breast sandwiches on top of swiss, I had to admit that the experience was good.

There was a liquor cabinet along the back of the box, and I wondered if it was included. I shrugged. I didn't sweat how much stuff cost...ever...including Majuscule.

So I took out two cold beers and handed one to Trouble.

"You're old enough to drink this now, right?" I asked him.

"Yeah, Dad." He shook his head. "How can you not know how old I am?"

"I feel like I've spent the last twenty years inside of a bad dream and just woken up." I cleared my throat. "I know that I should be more present in your life. I talked to the lawyers."

"Is something wrong? Is someone suing you?"

"No. Well, yes. But that has nothing to do with you." I wasn't going to talk to him about Majuscule and Star; we needed to keep it under wraps for now. "I was talking about our family's lawyers."

"Why?"

"I wanted to make sure that you were taken care of if I died."

"Morbid."

"I, uh, might have gotten mugged."

Trouble surged out of his feet, his fists clenched.

"What? When?"

"In Singapore."

"Singapore? Haven't you gone

there constantly?"

"Yes. You know that I'm frequently in Asia."

"The place where they don't allow gum."

"Yes, or guns. That's why I was surprised to find one pressed to my back."

"Holy shit, Dad."

I waved my hand. "It wasn't a big deal. I should actually thank him, but he took enough money to make it worth his while. I have been keeping things on an even keel, but it made me realize that my priorities haven't been right since your grandparents died."

"Grandma and Grandpa? What are you talking about? I barely remember them; I only know what they looked like because of pictures."

"I know." I looked down at the floor. "They loved you, you know. They didn't keep me in line like Adeline...your mother...did, but they made sure that I was there for you when I was around. After they died..."

"You weren't around," Trouble

finished. "I never connected that."

"The Flanagans loved you a lot. They were better parents than mine, and they were far better grandparents than I have ever been a father."

"But they died in that car crash when I was two."

I nodded. "That's right. I've been gone from your life for a long time. I just hope that we can make up for it. I know that you'll be busy pulling together your new life — trust me, I know what it's like to be a newlywed." I winked, and Trouble and I shared a grin full of masculine camaraderie. "But I also hope that you'll make time for me when I'm around in Los Angeles. Where are you going to live?"

Trouble had lived in dorm housing until recently, but he'd moved home each summer during college.

"I'm not sure yet. Laila surprised me when she decided to get married just like that, so I haven't given it much thought." He rubbed the back of his neck. "I guess that I should talk to real estate agents or something, because we'll need a place soon."

"Are you going to have kids?"

His jaw dropped. "I, uh, haven't though a lot about it."

"Well, you should."

"I just...that's a lot to think about, Dad."

"I had you. I wish that I'd had a dozen kids with your mother before she died."

"Well, you wish that she'd never died."

I nodded slowly. "Part of me is

buried inside of that casket, and I'll never get it back."

"I know."

"But life is for living. It may have taken me two decades to realize it, but I know that I want to be a bigger part of your life. I didn't know that you were serious enough about Laila to get married, or I would've given you your mother's ring. It's in a safe in the house. All you had to do was ask."

His jaw dropped. "What?"

"Yeah. It's still there. It's been

waiting for you."

"Well, Laila doesn't have an engagement ring, only a wedding band. The proposal, acceptance, and wedding all happened within the space of a few hours."

"I know."

"So I could still give it to her?"

"Yes, you absolutely could." I slapped him on the back. "I'll make sure to give it to you when we get home."

Just then, the national anthem played. We got to our feet and held our hands over our hearts as we listened. Then the game was in full swing.

I'd never really cared enough about baseball before to pay attention, but I had to admit that it was exciting in a way that football would never be for me. Trouble seemed to like it, and by the end of the second inning, both of our beers were empty. I was feeling pleasantly loose. Just some good company and a little beer were the components of a good afternoon.

"Excuse me," I told my son. My father, before he left, had always said that you didn't buy alcohol; you rented it. My bladder made it clear that the rented alcohol was ready to be set free.

Popcorn

Allen

I walked out into the main stadium in order to find restrooms. There didn't seem to be any in my section, but maybe I just didn't see them. I didn't like to ask for directions, so I just walked around in the hallways outside.

I finally saw a huge restroom sign and walked inside. For a sports stadium, the restroom was shockingly clean. I could see a clipboard near the door of the people who had initialed that they'd checked the bathroom, and it was checked on an hourly basis. I finished up there, and then I washed my hands.

When I walked back to my box, I was hit with the delicious scent of popcorn. I remembered what it was like to have that first date with Adeline every time that I smelled popcorn, but this time it didn't hurt. The memory was a good one, even though that date had started with Mr.

Flanagan threatening me and interrogating Adeline, making her late. I smiled. The good times with Adeline were excellent memories.

They didn't have buttery popcorn in the box, that was for sure. So I went and stood in the line to wait for some.

The couple in front of me was grousing about the prices.

"Sixteen dollars for a hotdog? Are you serious? Babe, I'd almost rather starve."

She bit her lip. "Maybe just

drinks?"

"Those are still six dollars! We can't afford that."

I could see tears in her eyes, and I tapped his shoulder.

He turned around and gave me a hard stare.

"What do you want?"

"Buy whatever you like. I'll pay for yours and mine. Don't argue with your lady. You should treasure the time that you spend together."

He blinked at me. "Do you mean that?"

"Every word." I guessed that he'd only really listened to the first part and not to the second, but his girlfriend or wife was staring at me with total adoration.

"You're a romantic, aren't you?"

I wasn't about to explain Adeline to random strangers, so I just said, "Yes."

She beamed at me, and I found myself engulfed in a hug. I didn't know what to do. Random strangers didn't hug billionaires in the normal course of things. I was wearing a long-sleeve t-shirt to cover my tats and shorts, so I guessed that it was somehow okay to hug random people when they were dressed casually. I didn't rub elbows with a large number of people that I didn't employ very often. I made a mental note not to do it anytime soon.

"Thank you!" she whispered in my ear. "We've been so worried about paying for my emergency hysterectomy, and I wanted to have a nice afternoon out. But he was upset about the babysitter and the cost of the tickets...and now the food...and you've made it all better, if just for a little while."

"My pleasure," I assured her. Money was a strange thing. If you didn't have enough of it, you thought of little else. If you did, then it ceased to matter.

They ordered nachos, hotdogs, and sodas. I noticed that the soda that they got didn't have lids on them. Was that a thing in sports stadiums? I shrugged. I normally wouldn't stop at a place like this, so I didn't really care.

I went up to the counter and told them, "I'd like a large popcorn."

"We can only give you a medium," the guy behind the cashier said. "We're out. I sent someone down to our stockroom to get more kernels, but he just radioed to me that we're out down there, too. We're done for the day."

"Medium it is, then." I didn't care. I just wanted the taste and smell of popcorn so that I could turn back time.

"Damn it," I heard behind me.

There was a petite lady with dark skin stomping her foot.

"Excuse me? Is something wrong?"

"I've been waiting in line for popcorn, too. I can't believe that they're out."

"It happens." I handed my cash to the cashier, and the bag of popcorn was handed to me. I could see that only a couple of pieces were left inside of the popping machine.

A thought occurred to me. I'd

done a small random act of

kindness...why not do another one?

"Would you like to share my

popcorn?"

I looked around. "Are you here

with anybody?"

"No, I just wanted to go to a

Dodgers game while I was in town."

"So nobody's waiting for you to go

back to your seat? You can come

back to my box, if you like."

She was shaking her head.

"Come on. It's fine. The view is

good, and my son certainly likes it."

She stopped shaking her head. "Your son?"

"Yeah, Trouble."

"Man, I'd sure like to hear the story behind that name. Do you have a good one?"

"I'm just plain old Allen. Come back to the box and I'll tell you." I wafted the air towards her. "Doesn't that popcorn smell good? Isn't it delicious? Don't you want to have a few pieces? Can't you imagine the way that the buttery popcorn will taste?"

"Okay, just for a little while." She followed me back up to my box, and I smiled the whole way. She was a little feisty, but I had to admit that it definitely added spice to things. Most women tried to spend time with me, but she had no interest in casually dressed Allen. I had to admit that it was refreshing to have somebody not care about what I could give them. I had only lured her with popcorn. It was simple. I was sure that she wasn't with me just so that she could get what she wanted.

Empty Box

Allen

When the two of us got back into the box, Trouble was on his feet.

"Dad, I was just about to call you. I've got to go." He had a frown on his face and a furrow between his eyebrows.

"But I thought that we were going to have some bonding time," I protested.

"Laila's period is late. She's

freaking out, and I'm going to take her to the doctor or something."

I nodded. "Go take care of your family, Trouble."

He turned to look at the lady that I'd suddenly brought to the box.

"Who's this?" He looked her up and down; I felt a sudden wave of possessiveness.

"I'm Valentina," she said, extending her hand to him. He shook her hand.

"Sorry, Valentina. I've got to go."

"Bye, Trouble. Call me if you

need me," I said.

"You mean that?"

"Anytime," I told him firmly. I meant it, and he must have seen that in my eyes, because Trouble nodded before he left.

The ball game was still going on as Valentina took Trouble's empty seat. We were watching the game, but I wanted to know more about the lady who'd wanted popcorn enough to follow me back here. There was a ledge in front of us. The popcorn was in the exact center at the beginning, but I noticed that it was slowly inching in her direction every time that she reached for it. I didn't mind; I was glad to have a little company on this outing, since Trouble's wife apparently needed him. Adeline had had a pretty uneventful pregnancy besides the light spotting except for the fateful end, which meant I didn't know much about what could go wrong with a pregnancy. For that, I was very grateful.

I cleared my throat. "So, ah, Valentina, do you have a last name?"

"Baez," she said absently, still watching the game and eating popcorn. "Valentina Baez."

"You said something earlier about wanting to catch a Dodgers game while you were in town."

"Yeah, I'm only in a given place for a week before I move on."

"What do you do?"

"I'm a healthcare administration consultant. I got my PhD in industrial engineering."

I did a double take and looked at her, really looked at her, again. She was a tiny thing, probably around 5 feet tall, and she could pass as a teenager if she wanted. It was surprising to me that she had a PhD.

"Dr. Valentina Baez?"

She smiled and chuckled just a little. "I don't use it, except for conferences and sometimes professionally."

"What does industrial engineering have to do with healthcare administration? I thought that industrial engineers dealt with factories."

"They do, but it's not all that we do. We handle everything that has to do with workflow. My job is to come into hospitals that have been reviewed by JCO as needing improvements and fixing their processes. I sometimes have longer-term contracts, but I generally come in, review everything and everybody for the first three days, and then I spend the fourth day in a ton of meetings with a bunch of recommendations given to key stakeholders."

"And what happens on the fifth day?"

"I go home," she said simply.

"Where's that?"

"Guess."

"DC?"

"Nope."

"Atlanta?"

"No."

"Okay, I give up."

"Indianapolis."

"What?" I looked her up and down. "You don't look like a farmer."

She snorted. "I'm not a farmer.

Indianapolis is one of the largest cities in the United States. Barely anybody knows that."

I didn't know that. I was California born and bred, and I had never been to the Midwest in my entire life. I was too busy doing deals in California and Asia to see much of the United States.

"That's interesting. I've never been to the Midwest."

"Yeah. It's funny to see the culture shock that you get coming from a smaller city to a mega-metropolis like LA. Your traffic is crazy and terrible. I use taxi drivers when I can."

"I don't blame you. There's a huge mix of driving styles here." I paused for a beat. "So you're in town for just this weekend?"

"Yes," she said quietly with a small smile. "I've got a flight to Seattle that leaves on Sunday night. I have to go in and review a hospital system and their doctors...I forget which system."

"It all runs together, doesn't it? If

you travel so much."

"Twice a week if I'm lucky," she said, her smile fading a little. "More if I'm not."

"So you're in high demand, then?"

"I specialize in certain things that other people don't do. Yes, I guess you could say that I am in high demand."

"Do you ever get lonely, traveling twice a week?" I went on plenty of business trips, but my bed was rarely empty if that happened. Valentina didn't look like the kind of women who fell into bed with men like me. For one, she couldn't possibly be a blond with impeccable hair, flawless clothing, and high heels, not in this stadium. She had the shoes for a Dodgers game, but she was wearing business attire with her hair pulled back into a small chignon at the back of her head.

She shook her head. "I'm a hermit," she explained. "I get plenty of interaction during the day, believe me. I have a family who loves me. I

FaceTime them a lot, but I don't need to live with them."

"You love them more at a distance, is that it?"

She smiled at me, and I felt warm as if I were being hit by sunbeams. "Yes."

My situation was a little different, but I felt as if Valentina could understand the choices that I made when I had left Trouble behind.

"Do you have any kids?"

Her back stiffened. "No."

"Married? Engaged?"

"Single. When you travel every week, there's not much of an opportunity to establish a relationship. When I'm home, I get to do the fun work of washing all of my clothes and trying to find enough groceries to keep myself alive until I go again. I don't date very often."

I gestured at the empty box. "This is a date."

She shook her head. "It's not."

"It is," I countered. "Look around. It's the two of us, a box with reflective one-way glass to ourselves. My son is gone. It's very romantic. Don't chicks dig that?"

"This chick doesn't," she said. "You're not going to impress me by showing off how much money you have. You convinced me to come up here to eat popcorn, and all of it is gone now." She showed me the empty container. "So thanks for the popcorn."

She got to her feet and started walking towards the door.

Dinner

Allen

"You're having dinner with me tonight."

She spun around.

"What?"

"We're having dinner. Right now."

"Are you crazy? We just met. And you haven't even asked me out."

"Will you go out with me?" I gave her my most charming grin, the one with teeth, the one that had convinced girls to fall into my bed for my entire life.

"No." She turned back towards the door, and I quickly darted around her to stand between her and it.

"Come on. One dinner. If you hate it, you can leave and never look back. You're only in town for this weekend. One dinner, please."

She sighed. "Well, that popcorn wasn't enough to fill me up. It was just a snack. Do you want to stay until the end of the game?"

"Only if you want to. Baseball is

not a particularly interesting thing for me; I just wanted to come with Trouble. If you want to leave now, we can just go. I know an Italian place that you might like."

Her eyes lit up. "I love Italian."

"Then we'll go there. Since we're both going, I can just drive you there and then come back to the stadium when it's empty. Less hassle that way."

"I'm not getting into a car with you. How do I know that you're not an ax murderer?"

"Do I look like one?"

She looked at my clothes. "No, you look like a middle-aged accountant who snuck out in the middle of the day."

"That's just about right." A billionaire accountant, but an accountant nonetheless.

"Come on. Live a little. Do something outside of your comfort zone."

She hesitated, and I sensed that she was crumbling.

"I'll pay for whatever wine you

want."

"You're going to regret that, buddy. I live pretty simply, but I love wine. I'm going to be ordering the most expensive one."

"Absolutely fine." I didn't care how much that wine cost. What I cared about was the pleasure of her company, and it sounded like she would let me take her there.

We walked out of the stadium together. I could feel my heart beating a little faster when I noticed the sway of her hips when she walked. She was wearing some kind of high-heeled boot, and it made her hips sway in her skirt. I had to admit that I couldn't stop watching the swing of her hips as we walked through the parking lot. I hit the button on my key fob, which made the headlights light up.

"You have a Roadster?"

"You like it?" A lot of my colleagues had Model S cars now, but I was happy with what I had.

"It's almost impossible to get one now. You have to buy them used, since Tesla stopped making them."

"I know. Have you ever ridden in a Tesla?"

"No."

"Well, climb in."

She scurried around the car as if she couldn't wait to try it out. I smiled. She was sweet.

I opened the door on my side of the car and got in. The Roadster came to life, and soon we were on the freeway and heading towards Il Segreto.

When we got there, it was mildly

busy but not overwhelmingly so.

"Two," I told the host, Eugenio.

"Who is this lovely lady?" he said,

looking Valentina up and down.

"Valentina," she said.

"What a pretty name," he told

her. "Come. We'll seat you at Mr.

McKane's favorite table."

My table was the one in the

corner. It was very small, just barely

enough for two people, and they only

used it when they were at capacity,

which meant that I could snag it

when I was here. It was in the back

corner of the restaurant and offered a vantage point and an easy trip to the bathrooms.

Valentina and I took the menus when Eugenio handed them to us along with the wine list. Valentina opened her menu.

Her jaw dropped.

"What in the world! This food costs more than my groceries for a week."

"Do you not like it? Should we go somewhere else?"

"I've never been here before, so I

don't know. But I do know that this place is crazy expensive. You didn't have to bring me here."

"You said you liked Italian. This is an Italian place."

"This place is about three or four times more expensive than a normal restaurant."

I shrugged. I knew I wasn't much to look at while I was wearing my casual clothes. "The food is good."

Valentina shook her head. "It better be encrusted with gold for the prices that they're charging."

"Do you want to get gold-flecked champagne then?"

She yelped, "No!"

Champagne

Valentina

This man was all kinds of crazy. Who drank gold? All you did was get rid of it!

"Let's just get normal champagne." Normal champagne. I shook my head. This whole thing was crazy.

"If that's what you want."

"I'm going to just go with the Italian wedding soup. I've never had a bad version," I said.

"Sounds great. I think that I'm going to go with penne fra diavolo."

"You like breathing fire?"

He smiled at me. "Yes."

I turned back to my menu. This whole conversation was weird and surreal. Somehow, he'd talked me into having a date that I wasn't too sure about. I had to admit, though, he certainly knew how to treat a girl.

On the other hand, plenty of men that I'd dated had started out at the classy places, just trying to impress me and show off how much money that they made. They thought that telling me that they made $80,000 a year would make my panties drop.

It didn't work like that.

One, I had a pretty good job myself. I had enough to cover my bills and put a little bit in a savings account. A lot of my expenses were business expenses since I traveled so much.

Two, no man was going to impress me with his salary, even if he made a million dollars a year.

That was the reason I was going for soup.

Allen motioned to a waiter who came straight to our table to take our order. The waiter brought over someone else, the sommelier, who talked to Allen about wine. I didn't know much about it, so I just kept quiet.

Then the waiter and sommelier were gone. Allen and I were left alone at the table. I started up the conversation again.

"So what do you do for a living?"

"I'm a businessman."

"Oh, that's interesting. What kind of business?"

"I invest in startups."

"Venture capital?"

"Yeah."

"I didn't know that there were that many startups in Los Angeles. I thought that they were all in San Francisco and San Jose."

"I've been up in San Francisco half the time and Singapore the other half for the past two decades."

"So you're rarely in LA? I was

lucky to catch you here, then."

"Yeah, you were. You're very lucky." There was something in his eyes, a spark of carnal heat, that made me shiver in my seat. He was promising me things with his voice that I wasn't sure if he could deliver.

I steered away from the talk of getting lucky, although I had to press my thighs together and rub them a little bit, feeling a little wetness between my thighs. It had been a long while since I'd gone to bed with anybody. Allen just might be the guy to cure my dry spell.

"What kinds of startups? Any that I would've heard of?"

The waiter came to our table with little focaccia buns with sun-dried tomatoes on top and a tiny bowl with olive oil with herbs in it. We began to eat our bread, tearing off little chunks at a time and dipping it into the olive oil. If I wasn't careful, I'd be full before our entrees arrived.

"I've invested in Star. You may have heard of it. It's sort of the star performer in our arsenal."

I dropped my bread on the table, leaving a grease stain where the oily part hit the tablecloth.

"You own part of Star?"

"It's included in one of my funds, yes. What, you've heard of it?"

"Yeah, I have. I work in healthcare, after all, and I was just looking at a mobile app on Android that focused on improving patient experience during inpatient stays."

"Oh, yeah? What does that have to do with Star?"

"Well, they showed me how it was

integrated with Star. They apparently just dropped some code in and were able to use Star's API, whatever that is."

"Yeah, that's how it works. Star is very easy to adopt."

"They were complaining a little about it, though."

He perked up. "Why?"

"It seems that Star takes about a day to process payments, and they want it to be instantaneous."

"We're working on it." He sighed. "The scale has gotten huge very fast, and with financial stuff it's better to be safe than sorry. So we're processing payments as fast as we can, but there's a queue."

I nodded. "Yeah, I'm sure you guys are getting slammed. The developers seemed pretty excited about how easy it was to implement Star's code in their own mobile app."

"Yeah, it is. Why do patients need to use Star?"

"Paying for extra stuff. Paying their bill before being discharged. There are lots of times that patients need something that will rack up a bill. Hospitals spend a fair amount of money chasing down patients who need to pay their medical bills; sometimes they go into collections. It's crazy, because a lot of hospitals will set up some kind of payment plan with the patients before it goes to collections, but they can't pay. Because of MTALA, hospitals have to stabilize patients who come to the emergency room no matter what, and a lot of the time, it's a wash. A write-off. A lot of hospitals have closed their emergency rooms as a result."

"Wow, I had no idea. That's a shame. Hasn't it helped that healthcare insurance is now mandatory?"

"It's helped somewhat, but there are still plenty of people who haven't signed up for healthcare, even with the subsidies."

He shook his head. "Somebody should fix that."

I smiled. "People are trying to do it. Smart people. There are a lot of healthcare systems that have started providing their own insurance inside of their own network. If you're in a certain area and pretty sure that you'll stay there, you can choose to go with a hospital system that will take care of you."

"What if you have an emergency and need to go to a doctor while you're on vacation?"

"They've all got policies in place for that; if you're admitted to the hospital when you go to the emergency room, you only pay a small co-pay. You foot the bill if you aren't admitted to the hospital. They definitely want you to only use it if it's necessary, but it's there if you really need it."

He nodded. "Maybe I should look into the healthcare sector. I've been focusing on finance."

"Half of a hospital's workflows are about billing and making sure that it's correct." I didn't know if that was an overestimate, but it sounded right. "Believe me, healthcare touches deeply on finance. Everybody needs healthcare, but not everybody can pay."

"I really should look into that. It's not right that there are any uninsured people at this point." He stroked his chin. "I'm going to make a note of that." He took out his phone and typed out a quick note.

"Going to look into it later?"

"My executive assistant will. She does preliminary research. I would need to look at companies in that space first, get a feel for what's going on."

"Interesting." I smiled at him. "So

you mostly focus on startups that have to do with finance?"

"Yes. The banking system is highly regulated, but it's overdue for an overhaul. There are a lot of startups working on bringing it into this century, some more successfully than others. I spent a lot of time with bankers, but it's worth it. When you stand next to a waterfall, you get wet."

"What does that mean?"

"When there is a lot of money flowing by you, you're going to get some of it."

I laughed. "I like that. Stand next to a waterfall, get wet. I'll have to remember that."

He smiled back at me, a smirk on his lips, and I knew what we were both thinking about.

Eating

Allen

Just when the conversation got interesting, our waiter came back with our food. The sommelier brought an ice bucket with a new bottle of Dom Perignon, then he uncorked it and poured it into our wine glasses. The waiter whipped out a small cheese grater.

"Would you like any freshly grated Parmesan with that? Pepper?"

"No, thank you," both of us said.

"Please don't hesitate to call me back." Tipping the waiters well was the key to having prompt service. He gave us a nod and then walked away.

"Your food smells really good," I told her. "What's in that?"

"Italian wedding soup is a mix of everything healthy and delicious. Would you like some?" She put her spoon in it and aimed it at me. Our eyes met and caught as she guided the soup spoon into my mouth.

I swallowed. "Mmm. Never had

anything better."

She was blushing a little and tucking a strand of hair behind her ear when she looked down at her soup and began eating it. I started eating my penne fra diavolo. Just like the name said, it was incredibly spicy.

The trick to eating spicy food and not totally embarrassing yourself during a meal, especially a date, was to put ice on your tongue. I drank some of my ice water straight from the glass and put an ice cube in my mouth. Was it easy to eat around an ice cube? No, but my masculine pride demanded it. I wasn't about to start crying in front of this woman. I wouldn't cry in front of the kind of woman who was making me hard just sitting there.

We ate in silence for a little while, each drinking a few glasses of the wine. Il Segreto really hadn't remained a secret for very long at all. She had eaten all of her soup and my penne fra diavolo was gone when a waiter came to our table with a dessert menu.

"Would you care for dessert today?"

I did, but it wasn't going to be found in this restaurant.

"I'm stuffed," Valentina said.

"I'll just take the check, please. In fact, here, just take this. Keep it for the tip."

The waiter's eyes bugged out as he registered that I'd given him about three times what the meal actually cost.

"Thank you, sir."

"Anytime." I probably wouldn't be quite so generous if I weren't in a hurry to get Valentina out of here.

The two of us got to our feet and headed for the door. I opened it for her.

"Thank you."

We walked to my car, and I felt strangely nervous, almost as nervous as I had been on the first date with Adeline. At least Valentina's father wasn't threatening me, though there was still time for that.

We got into my car when

Valentina said, "You know, I think that the game just ended."

"Oh?"

"Yeah, the parking lot is going to be a nightmare."

I began to grin. "So I should just drive you home? You'll grab the car tomorrow?"

"It's a rental, so I don't really care what happens to it. My credit card is specifically geared towards people like me, so they have car rental insurance baked in if I use it when I'm renting the car."

"I'll take you back to your hotel. Where is it?"

It was only about five minutes away. I took the turns a little fast while we went there, but Valentina didn't say a thing.

I parked in the parking lot.

"Let me walk you in."

She gave me a look. We both knew where tonight was going. I'd give her a chance to say no...but after that, she was going to be mine tonight.

We both got out of the car. The

Tesla locked itself as I got further away from it and we went through the back door of the hotel, the one leading to the big parking lot. We walked swiftly to a bank of elevators, which Valentina unlocked with her key card. It took us up to the fifth floor.

Then we were turning around the corner. Valentina swiped her card in the lock and pushed it open. With one foot in the door, she asked me, "Would you like to come...?"

She never got to finish that

sentence.

First Night

Allen

My mouth was on hers, claiming her, plunging my tongue inside of her mouth, mimicking what I was going to do to the rest of her.

Her hands were in my hair, pulling me down. I didn't mind the height difference. I just pulled her up by her waist. She wrapped her legs around me as our tongues danced, and I moved forward a step to keep the door open.

We needed to go inside the room now before some innocent hotel employee saw us fuck in the hallway. I walked forward with her in my arms, never disconnecting our mouths. I'd been hard for so long, and I felt myself getting harder as I smelled her scent and tasted it inside of her mouth. I couldn't remember the last time that I felt so aroused. The arousal was like a lion clawing at my insides. It wanted things, primal things.

I opened my eyes and saw a bed, and I walked towards it. I sat down on it. Now her legs, which were wrapped around me while we were standing, unwrapped so that her knees touched the bed. She was grinding on me now, pushing her sweet core against the spot where I needed it. But we were both fully clothed.

I needed to fix that. First, I took off all of her clothes. I threw them off of the bed, leaving them in a pile on the floor.

Then I maneuvered her so that her back was on the mattress. I kissed the tops of her breasts, feeling her breathing change before I took off all of my own clothes.

"You have tattoos. What kind of accountant has tattoos? They look like gang tattoos."

"They are gang tattoos." I didn't give her a chance to ask more questions. My hunger for her was driving me far too fast to discuss my past. There'd be plenty of time for that later.

I parted her thighs and aimed straight for her pleasure center. Her hips were writhing in no time, her hands twisted in my hair, bucking wildly into my face. She acted like my tongue was doing incredible things to her, and my finger penetrated her softness, dripping onto the sheets. Her thighs were starting to clamp around my head to hold me in place, so I went to heighten her pleasure by putting some of her cream on my pinkie finger and putting it in her back door.

She squeaked, "Holy shit!"

But then she was jerking in front of me, and I knew that she had orgasmed. Her inner muscles were clenching around my finger; I couldn't wait to feel her around my cock.

I had waited for long enough. I pulled her legs over my shoulders and stared straight into her eyes when she opened them. I took one hand and guided myself inside of her wet opening.

I slid inside without any

resistance.

"Oh," she breathed. "Oh."

My hand came down to touch her clit, and she bucked so hard that she almost took her legs off of my shoulders. But I moved my hands to keep them there. Her mouth was open and her eyes were closed, so I knew that she loved the feeling of me moving inside of her. She looked gorgeous beneath me as she shuddered in ecstasy.

But I lost the ability to concentrate on her as my body began to make demands. My blood was pumping while I thrust inside of her again and again, smelling her scent in the air. She was shouting now as she clenched around me yet again, so I began to spill inside of her luscious body, grunting a little as I released. The world went black around me.

When I opened my eyes, hers were still closed. She was trying to catch her breath as I took her legs off of my shoulders. I pulled out and lay on my back on her right side.

"That was amazing."

"Thank you."

"Thank you," she told me. "Man, I've never felt anything like that."

I traced the curve of her hip with one hand.

"Me neither."

Both of us were wet and sticky from our activities. I knew that I needed to shower.

She was coming with me.

First Shower

Allen

I got to my feet even though my thighs were still trembling a little in the aftermath of my orgasm. I leaned down and picked her up in my arms.

"Allen! I'm too heavy! Put me down."

"You're not too heavy. I carried you earlier." I walked towards the bathroom despite her protests. I saw that she had a shower, but it had a ledge in it that was the perfect height for shower sex.

I stepped inside with her in my arms. In order to turn it on, I needed to put her on her feet, so I did. I turned on the warm water, spraying everywhere. I reached for the soap and told her, "I'm going to wash you."

She watched as I lathered the soap in my hands before touching her. I started at her neck, worked my way down to her shoulders, went under her armpits and around her arms.

Then came the fun part.

I knelt in front of her. At this height, my face was right at her breasts. I sucked on each one in turn before washing it off. I kissed her cleavage before washing her there, too. She made little sounds that let me know that she enjoyed it.

Then I was kissing my way down her soft stomach, near her center. I washed her abdomen and made sure that the soap was gone before I went between her legs to eat up more of her delicious honey.

"Allen!" she exclaimed, her knees buckling a little. I caught her hips and pinned her against the wall with my tongue forcefully fucking her. She was shaking now, so I knew that it wouldn't be long. I used long strokes, drawing out as much pleasure as I could.

And sure enough, it wasn't. She cried out as she fell over the edge. I didn't know how many orgasms she'd had, but I knew that she'd never forget this night.

I turned her around so that her

front was crushed against the wall.

"I'm going to fuck you now," I told you. "Rough. Hard. Fast. Tell me now if you want it."

"I want it."

That was all of the permission I needed. I kicked her legs apart before pushing inside of her. She was moaning, and I shoved against her back until she was pressed very hard against the tile of the shower.

"Feels good, babe," I told her as I pounded away behind her. To make sure that she'd orgasm again, I went to touch her clit, rhythmically stroking it in time with each thrust of my cock.

She was bracing herself against the shower wall with her forearms and making incredible noises, noises that made me speed up and fuck her faster.

Then her whole body trembled as she exploded around me, screaming louder than before, milking me into my own orgasm. I filled her body with my seed.

I withdrew from her and spun

her around so that I could hold her in my arms while I sat down on the ledge.

"I'm pretty sure that I'm not that much cleaner," she told me.

"Nonsense. You're way cleaner after I put soap all over you. But there's one spot that I should probably check again."

"Oh?"

I took the bar of soap again, lathering my hand before I thrust two fingers inside of the wet hole that I'd recently vacated.

"Oh!"

Her eyes closed while her chin tilted up. I bit her neck a few times before focusing on using my thumb to stimulate her clit and push inside of her, hitting her g-spot over and over again. She rode my fingers so hard that a bottle of shampoo went crashing onto the ground, but I didn't care. She pulled my head so that I was kissing her as she jerked in yet another orgasm.

And then she was done, body trembling, her head going to the side in order to rest on my shoulder.

"All good?"

"I'm exhausted."

I couldn't deny that there was a sense of masculine pride in making her orgasm so often.

"Let's get you dried off, babe."

I quickly soaped myself up and rinsed off, then the two of us got out of the shower, wrapping ourselves in the thick white hotel towels before going back to bed. I could see the clothing that we'd discarded in the heat of passion; I thought they looked decorative. I'd like to see more of her clothing on the floor next to my bed, in fact.

The thought chilled me a little. I always broke off relationships when women were around too often, when it became normal for them to be there.

But Valentina was only here for a short time, anyway. She had this weekend, then she'd go up to Seattle for another contract. I had nothing to worry about.

I looked at her. She was yawning

like a baby kitten.

"Tired?"

"I'm wiped out. I'm not used to sex-athons, Allen."

I pulled her into my arms so that we were spooning. I kissed her shoulder before saying, "You better rest. There's more where that came from." I nudged her ass with my half-erect cock so that she knew what I was talking about.

"Put that thing away," she told me. "I can't take any more of it."

"We'll see what you're saying

tomorrow morning." I could order room service. In fact, we could order room service for every meal. I had no intention of letting her out of this room until she had to leave for her flight out of LA and out of my life. And if that thought somehow made my chest ache a little, so be it.

Poker

Valentina

When I woke up the next morning, the first thing I saw was Allen's head on the pillow next to mine. He was gorgeous, especially naked. I liked the thread of silver at his temples and reached for him to pull him in for a kiss.

He kissed me tenderly before he told me, "You snuffle in your sleep. It's not a full snore, just a light one...or heavy breathing." He tucked a strand of hair behind my ear. "It's cute. It's just like what Adeline used to do."

"Adeline?"

His expression changed. I felt like a cloud had covered the sun. "My dead wife."

He got out of bed and went into the bathroom. I heard the shower turn on.

Wow, I'd obviously touched a sore spot. It was probably best to leave it alone.

* * *

That night, we bought a pack of playing cards from the small convenience store in the hotel. We were playing poker while drinking all of the liquor in the mini-bar, but we were not playing for actual money. Each of us had a stack of IOUs, some of them sexual, others not. He was losing badly, and I couldn't tell if he was doing it deliberately because he enjoyed it or because I was a very good poker player. Probably deliberate, since I normally got cleaned out whenever I tried to play poker. I was pretty sure that he was trying to deliver on all of the sexual IOUs this weekend.

I had a royal flush in my hand, but he kept raising the stakes. They went higher and higher until the last card was turned.

"All in."

I blinked. "I really don't think you want to do that."

"Whatever, bluffer! Call or up the stakes. I'll enjoy taking all of those IOUs," he said, one eyebrow arched.

I called.

He laughed.

I showed him my cards.

The smile dropped off of his face.

"Thank you, I'll take all of those."
Now I had all the IOUs on the table. I
flipped through them. We'd written
them out before the game started,
filling them with things that we
wanted the other person to do.

I found one that I wanted him to
do. "Tell me a secret," I read aloud. I
looked up at him. Maybe it was the
wine talking, but I knew which secret

had been haunting me all day.

He just looked at me, his eyes wary.

"I want to hear about Adeline."

He picked up his glass and drank the rest of the wine in it.

"You really want to know?"

"Yes."

"It's a long story."

I turned my palms up and shrugged. "We've got as much time as you like."

He turned and put his wine glass on the ground.

"Let's get comfortable, because this is going to take a while."

We both got back into bed. He put his head on my breasts and an arm around my waist. Warmth spread in my chest from our intimate position, and I put my arm around him as he began to tell me his story.

II. Past

Adeline's Death

Dealing

Allen

MORE THAN TWENTY YEARS AGO

I checked my Rolex. Adeline had called me on her private line last night to have me meet her after school. Like me, she was 19. Unlike me, she was still in high school. I'd opted out of high school when I turned 16 and took the CHSPE. I didn't care about school, even though I'd always gotten good grades. My friends called me a nerd, and school was insanely boring for me. I spent most of my time reading books under my desks. I always did well on standardized tests, but my teachers said that I didn't live up to my potential. I constantly disrupted class just to have something to do.

So I was just as relieved as my teachers when I'd gotten my results back from the test. I'd sobered my mom up enough to drag her to school to present my certificate and formally announce that I was leaving. At 16,

I'd taken to the streets.

My mother was an alcoholic, not the kind of woman who just had a little wine with dinner. Our liquor cabinet was always stocked, and we lived down the block from a seedy liquor store with a half-broken sign. Only part of the neon sign lit up. But she was down there every afternoon picking up more.

When I turned 18 and became a legal adult, I stopped caring about what she did. I would make my own way. Though she didn't hold down a job, she got Social Security Disability payments that paid the rent, kept the lights on, and provided groceries. She said that she had anxiety, and I didn't ask questions as long as I still had a home with running electricity. She didn't have a job; she said that she couldn't keep one without having panic attacks.

There aren't that many things to do for a 16-year-old boy who has nothing to do but watch cable TV. I'd started hanging out with the other 16-year-olds in my neighborhood, and a lot of them belonged to gangs.

I looked at their nice watches, their chains, and hot cars. The babes weren't too bad, either, so I joined one. I had two full sleeves of tattoos showing that I belonged to someone; I normally wore sleeveless shirts to show them off. I accessorized with reflective aviators and bandanas. I belonged somewhere with people who cared about me, something that I'd never really gotten from my mother, who was drunk more often than not. And so what if I'd stolen a car or a dozen of them? Okay, more like three or four dozen. It was easy money, and hot-wiring a car wasn't rocket science. Neither was using a wire coat hanger to open locks.

After a bunch of my gang had been taken off to juvie in a car heist gone wrong, where Gino had killed someone, the rest of the gang switched to something a little safer: slinging marijuana and cocaine plus a few other things to the teenagers at the richest high schools in the area. In the power vacuum that was created when Gino left, I'd taken the reins. It wasn't hard. Nobody else wanted to track all the shipments and figure out what needed to go where. They'd take direction: take this shipment here, go there, find this person, etc. But logistics weren't their strong suit, so I kept track of it all and made the wheels turn.

I was the one who figured out how to get the best market share when selling drugs. We had to target the people who could pay enough to make it worth our time. We didn't find those people in our own neighborhoods. We found the cosseted and coddled teenagers whose parents gave them black AmEx Centurion cards and kept drawers of unlimited cash in the house. They existed at the prep schools in the area.

Adeline was one of them. I'd been dealing to her for years. She was pretty, long white-blond hair with bright blue eyes, and I had to admit that I gave her all of her cocaine at cost just to see her more often. We saw each other once a week at least, almost like a date. I'd been too shy to ask her out, because she was a knockout, but I'd do it some day.

She looked as beautiful as a doll, always immaculate. I had blond hair and blue eyes, too, but I didn't look anything like her. She hid her habit very well, except that she was just a little too thin, since cocaine stole her appetite. She said that she had to keep using it to fit into her dresses, but I was starting to worry a little bit about the way that her collarbones poked out so much. Her elbows didn't look that great at this point, either.

I heard the hum of her sleek silver BMW convertible, and I breathed a sigh of relief. Though I hadn't admitted it to myself, a corner of me wondered if she would blow me off. Half of my clients did at some point, and I always charged them double from then on.

That's another thing about the pipeline: we protected our territory, so the rich snobs had to go through us to get their fixes. We could charge anything at all, and the money that we'd made had been invested in spreading out, getting more inventory, acquiring more customers, etc. We had all of the private schools on lock, but the public schools had plenty of people like us, those willing to take a risk in order to make the solid profit, so we kept away from them. Once in a while, a scholarship kid at one of the private schools would try to undercut us.

That was fine. We were kind and merciful. We slashed the tires of his family vehicle as a warning. If he didn't stop, he'd find some other things slashed. All of them so far had stopped after finding their tires slashed.

She got out, pretty as a picture. She was wearing a lovely black dress with blue and white flowers on it. The neckline of her dress dipped low, and my eyes were drawn to the shadow between her breasts like she had a magnet there.

"Hi, Allen. How was your day?"

"Hi, Adeline. It was good." I

offered her my arm. She took it, and then we went into a nearby alley. I liked feeling the gentle touch of her delicate hand on my arm.

"You've got it," she said, licking her lips.

"Yup." I took a small baggie of cocaine out of my pocket and handed it to her.

She looked at the small baggie in her hand. "I wish that you could give me more than one kilo at a time."

"Most people can't afford even that much."

"I'm not one of those people." Her father was an executive at one of the huge studios, Phim Bros., and to me, he seemed to have more money than Croesus.

I also would admit that the one kilo limit was only for Adeline. As soon as she used up all of her cocaine, she had to call me and meet me again.

"Adeline!"

Both of us turned towards the entrance of the alley, and a man who looked like Adeline was coming through. His hair was turning more white than white-blond, but he was practically breathing fire.

"Adeline, is that cocaine? I knew it." He came towards her, his hand reaching to take the full, white baggie

.

I turned and ran the hell out of that alleyway, my heart pounding as I sprinted as fast as I could. I had no desire to tangle with Adeline's father; if he confiscated all of my cocaine, I'd be out of all the money that I should make today. I'd already lost the money that Adeline should've paid

me, but I'd consider myself lucky that

I was able to get out before he had

called the cops.

Phone Call

Allen

THREE MONTHS LATER

I looked at the phone ringing in my hand. I had called Adeline every day after that day in the alley, but she'd never picked up. Then I'd called every other day, and now I was calling on a weekly basis. I knew that her private line was in her bedroom, so it wasn't going to be picked up by anybody else, including their staff. It rang and rang. Where was she?

I gasped when I actually heard Adeline's voice say, "Hello?"

"Adeline?"

"Allen?"

"Are you okay? What happened to you?"

I could hear little gasps that told me that she was crying.

"My parents put me in rehab for three months."

"Man, that's rough." Secretly, though, I was glad that they'd cleaned her up, even though she didn't have a reason to see me anymore. I'd figure out a way around that.

"No one will talk to me anymore. I don't have any friends," she whispered, then she hiccuped. "Everyone calls me a coke whore behind my back now."

"You're not a coke whore, Adeline. You just regularly used cocaine, that's all." Hell, tons of my gang brothers used drugs, though I didn't dip my hands in the merchandise. I'd rather sell inventory than use it; there was no profit to be made on cocaine that you took yourself.

"It doesn't matter what the truth is," she shouted into the phone. "Everyone thinks that there's something wrong with me."

"Adeline, this is LA. If you're not using drugs, you're doing something wrong."

She was crying again, and listening to her sobbing broke my heart.

"I can't..." she whispered. "I want

to die."

My heart went ice cold. "No, Adeline."

"I mean it! I feel like my parents are prison wardens or something. Rehab was awful, but my parents are even worse."

"You're 19. Just leave."

"I can't. They'll cut me off."

"I'll take care of you," I told her, with more confidence in my voice than I felt. But I was 19, and I knew that I loved her.

"You? You deal drugs, Allen. I

should be staying away from you. You're part of my addiction. That's what my therapists said."

"I can promise you that you'll never get drugs from me again," I swore to her. "They aren't good for you."

"You mean that?"

"I swear."

She sighed. "I really don't have any friends anymore."

"I'm sorry about that. You have me."

"My drug dealer?"

"Your friend. I'm not going to leave you just because you recently kicked a cocaine habit."

She sighed again. I could practically hear her thinking. "That's true."

"So how about it? Want to hang out?"

"What do you want to do?"

I didn't know what rich chicks like Adeline did. "Uh, go to the movies?"

"You don't know, do you? You've never been friends with a girl before, have you?"

"I'm willing to find out."

"You're really good looking."

"Thanks?"

"I mean, you've probably only taken girls out on dates."

"True." I didn't have any siblings, and I had only taken girls out on dates...if you called what I did "dating."

There was a little pause again, then she said, "I want you to take me on a date."

My heart leapt straight out of my

chest. I wanted to play it cool, but I did a huge fist pump that she couldn't see.

"Dinner and a movie?"

"That sounds nice," she said softly, her voice a little breathy. "But I'll meet you at the theater."

"I'll see you there."

"Seven at the one close to the school, okay?"

"I'll be there."

"Bye." The phone clicked as she hung up on her end. There was nobody in my room, so nobody could see me do a victory dance. I'd scored a date with the most beautiful girl I'd ever met, and I wasn't going to mess it up.

I knew that my normal sleeveless shirt and bandana weren't going to cut it. If I was going to take Adeline on a date, then I'd need to go shopping.

Shopping

Allen

I went to Rodeo Drive. I might be a dealer and somewhat of a thug, but I had cash to burn. A lot of cash, frankly. I couldn't go to banks, so I had everything in a safe in my closet, behind a secret panel that I'd installed. If anybody looked closely, they'd see it. But if you didn't look at the dimensions of my closet, then you wouldn't notice the fake panel that looked like a wall. It had been one of the first things that I bought with the money that I got from dealing.

I got a lot of suspicious glances from the clerks, but I didn't care. I had enough money to buy an entire wardrobe if I wanted to, but a shirt for today would do.

"Can I help you?" a supercilious store assistant asked, her tone verging on the edge of rudeness.

"I've got a date tonight. I'd like to be dressed well enough to take her out."

"And what's your budget?" the store assistant, whose badge said that her name was Kaelyn, asked me.

"Unlimited."

Her eyes went wide. "Oh."

"Yeah. So can we do this?"

She blinked a few times, then she turned and went swiftly to the back of the store.

"This is where we keep our highest quality shirts," she told me. I knew that "high quality" was a euphemism for "overpriced," but I'd take one anyway. I wanted to look good for Adeline.

"I don't understand colors or whatever." My mother had never taught me about clothes, and she didn't get dressed until the afternoon, anyway. I bought my own clothes, and I never asked her for style advice.

"I do," Kaelyn told me. She started picking shirts off of the rack and shoved them at me in a big bundle of large wooden hangers. "Go to the dressing room and try these on. I'll tell you which ones will work for you. You've got stunning eyes, you know." Her face came close to mine, and I leaned back. "It's like you've got blue stars with little lines in them for eyes."

"Yeah, I know." I saw my own face in the bathroom mirror every day. I knew what my eyes looked like.

"Go."

I went into the dressing room and pulled off my sleeveless shirt, tossing it on the ground. I slid into the first shirt. The fabric felt totally different from what I normally wore. It was stiffer. It was as if this dress needed to be starched or something. Damn, I had no idea about stuff like that. The sleeves gaped open at the end. I needed to find cufflinks or some shit.

I buttoned up the first shirt and came out for Kaelyn's inspection.

"Turn, sir." Oh, now that she was making a huge commission off of me, she'd actually be helpful and polite. I turned around.

"Good. Turquoise really works for you."

"I've got four more shirts to try on."

One by one, I put them on and wore them for her. She chose two of them, discarding three as "not your color," whatever that meant.

"I need pants, too."

"Slacks?"

"Whatever."

Kaelyn, extremely helpful now, went to a rack with simple black pants. I told her my measurements, and she gave me pants that should fit. I tried them on in the dressing room, but they were too short. I guessed that I'd grown since the last time that I cared. I mostly wore shorts, anyway. She came back with a longer size.

"You're six foot, aren't you?"

"Something around there," I told her.

"Well, try it on."

I went back into the dressing room. The fabric was thick wool, and I would stifle in the heat. But I wanted to impress Adeline, so I'd wear it anyway.

I came out in the turquoise shirt that I'd tried on first and the black pants.

Kaelyn's jaw dropped.

"Wow," she breathed. "You look so different."

I turned to take a look in the mirror. I looked like a businessman with a stick up my ass.

"Do you want a tie? A sports jacket?"

Would Adeline expect that? No, this was LA. It was too hot to wear an outer jacket. I didn't think that she'd particularly care about the tie.

"No, what I've got now is good

enough."

"Okay. I'll ring you up, then. Do you want to wear it out?"

I looked down at my wrists and remembered. "Do you have cufflinks?"

"You want just basic ones?"

"The best you've got," I told her firmly.

"I don't think you want those ones. They're made of vvsi diamonds."

"What does that mean?"

"It means that they're too

expensive for actual people to buy."

"Ring them up," I told her. I went back into the dressing room to get my shorts and shirt.

The assistant swallowed hard, then she scanned out my other shirt and grabbed a turquoise shirt and set of pants off the rack to get the right price. She named a sum that equaled about half a kilo of cocaine.

Her eyes bugged out when I brought out a huge stack kept together by a rubber band. I laid down Benjamins on the countertop, counting them out one by one. She put them under the cash tray after she'd counted them herself, and she handed me some change. I put it in another pocket, then I took the girly bag with swirly silver writing on the outside to my car. Maybe it was overkill to buy two shirts, but I could always hope that Adeline would let me take her out a second time.

First Date

Allen

I was sitting in my car with the windows down. It was a sweet 1967 Corvette, one that we'd taken and I'd been attached to from the moment that I laid eyes on it. It was mine.

I waited in the parking lot near the entrance looking for Adeline, but she didn't show.

7:15 passed, and she didn't show.

7:30, then, and she still didn't show.

The movie showtime was 8 — we hadn't checked the paper for showtimes — so we weren't going to be late. But there were now sweat stains under my armpits as I sat in the Los Angeles heat, waiting for a girl who wasn't coming.

Then I saw her silver BMW convertible with the hood up, and I stood and waved. It came right to me. She had tinted windows, and she rolled the driver's side window down.

I walked towards it and said, "Hey," before stumbling back a step.

The driver wasn't Adeline. It was her dad. She was sitting in the passenger seat, one finger nervously twisting in her hair.

"You're the boy who's dating my daughter?"

"Yes, sir." Dating was kind of a leap, but hell, I'd date her if she'd let me. Adeline was the kind of girl men dreamed about — pretty, sweet, and rich enough to take care of everything, not that I'd ever rely on her for money.

"Why didn't you pick her up at the house?"

"She told me to meet her here, sir." Was her dad going to put the kibosh on this before we ever went on our first date?

"I want you to know that I have a registered shotgun, son. And I'll be watching you. Get out, Adeline." Adeline opened her door, and she got onto the sidewalk. Her face was white.

"You better be clean, boy. I've

just spent a fortune cleaning up Adeline, and I don't have time to mess with some addict."

With perfect truth, I told him, "I've never snorted anything in my life, sir." Adeline turned to look at me, but she could hear the ring of truth in my voice.

Her dad scoffed. "Adeline comes home by 11. It's a school night."

"Yes, sir."

He pointed at me. "Make sure she's home by then."

It left no time for dinner, but I'd

handle it.

"Yes."

The convertible moved off, and I put my hand on Adeline's hip. I realized that she was trembling slightly.

"Are you okay, Adeline?"

She was crying now, the tip of her nose turning pink while tears dripped down her cheeks. I gave her a hug. "Hey, it's okay. You're just here for a movie."

"You have no idea," she sobbed, burying her face in my new turquoise shirt. I had to admit that I liked it, even though the tears were soaking through the thick material. Oh well, this shirt had to have the sweat cleaned out of it anyway. "I just sat through the longest interrogation ever."

I patted her back, noticing how soft she was and needing to adjust my pants a little. "Let's get tickets and go in, okay? We'll get popcorn with extra butter."

She wiped her eyes.

"Okay."

The two of us went up to the ticket counter and bought tickets to the show. It was a romantic comedy, and I hoped that it would put a smile on her face. I brought her to the ticket counter so that we could buy a huge tub of popcorn and get so much butter that we'd have a heart attack right there in the theater.

"I never get extra butter. My mom always yells at me when she thinks that I'm eating too much."

I touched her elbow, which thankfully had filled out a little while she'd been in rehab. "I don't care how much you weigh. I think that you're a beautiful person. You could weigh twice as much, and I'd still love you."

"You're sweet," she told me, and I knew that she didn't believe me. But it was the truth.

"Let's go get our seats."

She linked her arm with mine, and I loved how it felt to have her so close to me. She smelled nice, like flowers. I'd wanted to ask her out for a long time, but she was way out of my league. She was from a different world; I was just a visitor.

When we went into the movie, we were engrossed from the first few minutes. She laughed, and I knew that she was feeling better. She rested her head on my shoulder about halfway through the movie, and I felt like the luckiest guy in the world. I had to be sure to get her home by 11 to avoid her father's wrath, and I was planning on getting her home before then. But right now, I reached for her hand. She squeezed mine, and my pulse raced as I thought about kissing her.

It was funny, because I'd kissed plenty of girls. Gotten plenty of them naked, too. But the prospect of a kiss from Adeline was worth far more than any of that.

I started sweating again, but this time not from the Los Angeles heat; the movie theater had crazy air conditioning that was bringing out goosebumps on Adeline's arms. I hoped that she didn't notice. I used a little cologne before I left, but it wouldn't cover the smell of all the sweat, and I couldn't sniff myself without Adeline noticing.

Finally, the movie was over with a big, long kiss when the two characters finally found happiness together and bought a house with a white picket fence.

I stood as the lights came on. Adeline and I walked out, my arm around her waist. She didn't seem to mind. We got into my car, and it was 10:30.

"I better take you home."

"Okay."

"I don't know where you live," I told her, embarrassment clear in my voice. We'd never met there.

"I'll show you. Don't worry."

True to her word, she directed me through all the turns to get back. I sat there, parked in front of her house. I could see that the lights were on inside. Her parents were waiting for her.

"I had a really nice time tonight. Thanks for coming out with me." I turned to her to say goodbye.

Her face was really close to mine.

Was she trying to kiss me? Would she slap me if I leaned forward?

She stopped all the questions by moving forward a half centimeter and touching her lips to mine. She gave me a brief kiss, and I moaned a little. She was a good kisser.

"I've got to go. My parents are probably right at the door." She grabbed my hand and squeezed it before she got out of the car.

I watched as she went in the front door, then I backed out and left. I felt a little drunk from her kiss, even though it'd lasted one second, with a closed mouth, no tongue at all. Adeline had me twisted into knots. A light kiss from her was worth more than all of the sex with all of the girls that I'd ever had before.

Graduation

Allen

THREE YEARS LATER

Sitting in an uncomfortable folding metal chair, I adjusted the cap on my head. I couldn't make it sit right. I felt like a doofus in my stupid robes, but Adeline's parents insisted that we attend our graduation ceremony. My mother hadn't bothered to show up.

I still lived at home while I

attended USC. Adeline moved out of her parents' house and lived in the dorms, where I spent most of my evenings. She'd managed to get a single, and the two of us spent a lot of time together.

She might look like a sweet little doll, but she had the steel backbone of a general. When she'd realized that my grades and CHSPE degree were enough to get me into USC, along with a little pressure and a donation from her dad, she'd insisted that I attend the same university as her.

People like me didn't go to USC, but they did if someone like Mr. Flanagan said I did, so they'd let me in.

She bullied me into actually doing my homework. We were enrolled in all of the same classes. She wanted to get an accounting degree, and if she did, I was getting one, too.

We didn't spend our time together rolling around in her bed, as much as I would've liked for that to happen. She said that she wanted to save it for marriage, so I spent a lot of nights alone with my hand. I didn't mind. She was worth it.

We worked on all of our homework together, and because of her, I had the best grades that I'd ever gotten in my life. Her parents said that she could only get married after she had her degree, so she'd jam-packed our schedules to go through everything as fast as we could. We took extra courses over the summer. We didn't take any fun electives; she was all business. She said that one day she'd inherit some stock from her dad, so she wanted to understand what was going on. When she said "some stock," I got the impression that it was a lot of stock, probably more than I could wrap my head around, so I didn't pry.

As soon as we graduated, I was going to propose; I'd known that I would since we entered USC. Her dad had already given us his blessing. I had a ring in my pocket, bought out of the money that I'd saved tutoring people in the writing center. It had taken a lot of hours and a lot of essays, but I'd finally gotten enough to afford a small ring for her. It wouldn't be anything like her mother's, and I'd replace the stone later once I could afford it, but I'd gotten her mother to help me pick it. I knew that she'd like it. I was going to propose at dinner tonight.

Finally, the closing speech came. I went and moved my tassel, and everyone threw their hat in the air. I was glad to get the stupid thing off of my head, so I didn't even try to pick it up.

I made my way to the rendezvous point that Adeline had set. I stood there and waited, thinking about how I'd return the robes tomorrow.

Finally, I saw her make her way to me. I smiled and she ran into my arms.

"We did it!" Both of us had gotten jobs at Phim Bros. in their accounting department, thanks to Mr. Flanagan. Life was a lot easier when you had someone who could pave the way for you, and Mr. Flanagan, after years of holding out, finally approved of me, at least a little. He wanted to see his little girl happy, so I made sure that everything I did showed him that I was committed to her.

When I'd started dating Adeline, I'd cleaned up everything. I wore the clothes that her family expected me to wear. I talked the way that they talked. I walked with less swagger. I stopped hanging out with my friends, my brothers. They'd groused about some chick stealing me away, but they'd understood. I'd gotten a ticket out of my old life, and they weren't going to begrudge me my shot at making it out. I still had their backs, but I didn't run the show anymore. One of the younger kids was fine at writing stuff down, making sure that the wheels turned, and I put everything in his hands. I didn't have to worry about what happened when Gino got out because I was done. Done with all of it.

So Adeline and I walked to where we were supposed to see her parents, out by the parking lot. Adeline had

had a photo shoot yesterday with her wearing her robes and smiling at the camera. I didn't know what it was like to have parents who cared. My dad had disappeared when I was too young to remember him, which had contributed to my mother's decline. I had no memory of my mother holding a job, just going to the bank and cashing the checks that were only just enough to live on if we only bought the necessities and thought really hard about what those actually were.

Her dad caught my eyes when we were close to them, and I patted my jacket pocket, currently hidden under these hideous robes. He knew that I was going to propose tonight.

Proposal Dinner

Allen

TWO HOURS LATER

Rich people ate way fancier food than normal people ate. They had so many courses, too. At home, we'd have a bowl of salad on the side while we ate our mac and cheese, and that's about as fancy as we got. But after hanging around Adeline, I had to learn which fork to use when. It was a bunch of nonsense, but etiquette was important to her, so I learned whatever she wanted me to.

When the servers came to take away our desserts, I cleared my throat.

"I, uh, I've got something to say."

Mr. Flanagan leaned forward in his chair.

"Yes?"

I got on one knee next to Adeline. Her hands flew to her mouth, and her eyes were wide. I reached inside of my jacket to pull out a small jewelry box.

"Adeline Flanagan, you've been the brightest star in the sky for me for years. I've known that I wanted to marry you basically since we started dating. Would you do me the honor of marrying me?"

"Yes!" she shouted. The tables around us burst into applause. I put the ring on her finger, a ring that meant that we'd be together forever.

Though I'd never tell her, I was nervous that she'd say no. But we'd been together for the last three years, and I'd waited until she had her degree to do it, so her father had approved.

Adeline hugged me hard. Mr. Flanagan tossed some cash on the table and got to his feet to clap me on the back.

"Glad that you'll be part of the family, son." He leaned down and kissed Adeline's temple. "Can't wait to see you get married, love-bug."

"Daddy! I'm too old for that nickname."

"You're never too old for that nickname, kiddo. When you have gray hair, you'll still be my little love-bug."

She was blushing, but I knew that she liked the name that her dad called her.

"Let's go out for ice cream," I suggested. I knew that her mom watched her weight and Adeline's weight carefully, but it was a night for celebrating. We were old enough now to drink, but I felt uncomfortable doing it in front of Adeline's parents. It was better if we celebrated with ice cream.

"Let's go," Mr. Flanagan said.

"I'll go with Allen," Adeline said. I smiled. I knew what we were doing in the car.

"We'll see you there in 15 minutes," Mr. Flanagan said. He winked at me. The ice cream place was 5 minutes away, two if the lights were green.

Adeline held my hand as we walked out to the car. I started up the Corvette, then she leaned across the center console. I put my arms around her slender body as I kissed her hard, so hard that both of us were gasping for breath when I finally let her go.

"I want to be your wife," she told me. "I've wanted it for years."

"Your dad gave me his blessing as long as I waited for you to graduate. Your mom helped me pick the design of the ring. We can change the stone later."

She looked at it. "I'm happy with what I have. It's beautiful."

I leaned in and kissed her cheek. "We've got to hurry, or your parents will wonder where we are."

We went to the ice cream place to celebrate, and it was one of the happiest nights of my life.

Childbirth

Allen

NINE MONTHS LATER

"Push, baby," I told her. Adeline's forehead was covered in sweat. Her hair was sticking to it, and she looked absolutely exhausted.

"I can't," she gasped. "I just can't anymore."

"We can do it, baby. Just breathe like they taught you in those classes. Don't you want to meet Trevor

McKane? You'll be fine."

Her hand was squeezing mine so tightly that my fingers had turned white, but she was still obviously in pain. The baby had moved too quickly for her to get an epidural, and she was doing the whole thing without the drugs that we'd planned to use.

"Ah!" she screamed.

"The baby is crowning," announced the nurse. "Another big push and that baby will be out."

"Uh!" she shouted.

"And he's out." The nurse briskly moved forward. "Do you want to cut the cord?"

I never wanted to take scissors to any part of my wife's body, so I shook my head. She briskly cut the cord that connected Adeline and our baby.

He was slimy, covered in blood and placenta. His eyes were shut. The nurse briskly spanked him, and he screamed bloody murder. She did some other things, before she said, "His Apgar score is 6. Healthy."

"Thank goodness," Adeline said.

She squeezed my hand. "We did it."

"Yes, we did." I glanced at the bed. Was it just me, or did the pool of blood seem to be huge?

"Should we clean up the placenta and all that?" I asked the nurse.

"First, I've got to clean the baby. Your wife's body will expel the afterbirth. Be right back." She bustled out of the room holding our baby.

I held Adeline's hand and kissed her mouth softly. "I can't wait to go home with you and our baby."

"Me, either."

I touched her cheek. "You and the baby are the most important things in the world to me."

"Equally?"

"You know that you're always my number one, baby." I kissed her again. Her eyes closed, and her breathing was shallow. I guessed that she was really tired from this whole thing. She'd been in labor for a long time.

When we'd found out that she was pregnant, the doctor basically told me to force-feed Adeline milkshakes. She was too thin to sustain a pregnancy; we'd been scared to death when Adeline had spotted blood in her underwear during the second month of her pregnancy.

But we'd made it through, and our baby was healthy. That's what mattered.

I looked at the puddle that came out of Adeline, the one that was between her legs.

"Can't wait to get a look at all

that, eh?"

"Adeline, you're bleeding."

"It's normal," she reassured me. "It's okay."

"I don't know if I can go through this again," I told her. "I don't like seeing you in pain."

"We might get carried away..." Adeline said, her smile lighting up her eyes in the way that I particularly liked. Then her eyes closed as her head drooped to the side.

"We'll see." If I had any say, Adeline wouldn't have to go through this whole thing again. Maybe we'd adopt a baby. I had bad memories of the last days of my mother's life, as the cirrhosis killed her. She'd died a few months after we graduated, when I was just getting on my feet at Phim Bros., so she hadn't seen much of my adult life. She'd had a simple funeral and a cheap burial. I had all of her worldly possessions, which weren't much. We'd lived from check to check after all. I'd given up the apartment in the old neighborhood, and Mr. Flanagan had helped us find a house.

The puddle was growing larger, and I was really worried. Adeline was pale, and I didn't know if that was just exhaustion from the birth or what. I saw that her heart rate was high and her breathing was a little too fast. It was enough to make me drop her hand and head for the door.

Her eyes opened. "Where are you going?"

"To get a nurse."

I went to the nurse's station, and I rapped on the countertop until a nurse looked up from a patient's chart.

"Yes?"

"My wife is bleeding a lot."

"It's normal," she told me. "Don't freak out. It'll be over soon."

"Yeah, that's what they told us a long time ago."

She frowned. "Let me go in and check. She's not my patient, you know."

"I know. Just please come help."

She came into the room and saw my wife lying there in a big puddle.

"Holy mother of pearl!" She hit a

button that set off an alarm. She ran out the door. I heard her scream, "We need a doctor in here, stat!"

I watched helplessly as various nurses and doctors came into the room.

"She's lost too much blood," I heard them say. I stood in the corner as they hooked her up with a few units of blood.

"She won't stop bleeding."

"She's hemorrhaging."

"She must have torn part of her uterus. We can't get it to stop."

"I want coagulant stat."

The team around her was a total circus, in constant motion. I didn't know what was happening, so I just tried to stay out of their way.

I saw her heart monitor having smaller and smaller lines, until it was flat. I knew that wasn't good.

"She's coding," a nurse shouted. Even more people came into the room. I saw the electrical paddles that I'd only ever seen on TV. They were opening my wife's gown and applying it to her chest.

"Clear!"

They shocked her once. And again. And a third time, but her heart didn't start beating again.

She was dead.

Funeral

Allen

A few days later, I sat in the front pew at my wife's funeral. Her dad gave the eulogy. Her mother held my hand. It hurt to look at them. They looked like her.

After Adeline had died, I'd taken the baby to the Flanagans. Mrs. Flanagan knew what a baby needed better than I did. I'd brought all the stuff from the nursery over to their house, and Trevor had Adeline's old room now. I knew that he was in good hands, so I didn't come over every day. Or every other day. Or even every other weekend. It hurt to look at the baby who had stolen my wife from me. I knew that it wasn't fair to blame him, but it wasn't fair for my twenty-two-year old wife to die, either. I was too young to be a widower.

I hadn't been back to work since my wife had died. I drank and drank until I couldn't see anymore. I knew that my mother had died of cirrhosis, and these days, I wanted to die of it, too. I needed Adeline. She was the center of my universe, my shelter in the storm. Without her, I was nothing.

I was in the Flanagans' car when we went to the cemetery to watch my wife being buried in the cold dirt. Her mother was crying, and her father's face was set in grim lines. I said nothing, did nothing, just stood there while they shoveled dirt over the love of my life, the mother of my child, a child I could barely stand to look at.

"Do you want to pick up Trevor now? It's over," Mrs. Flanagan was asking me.

"Why would I?"

"He's your son."

"He's our son," I said, and my voice cracked. "Adeline's and mine. We were supposed to do this together."

"Do you want us to keep him?"

I nodded.

"How long?"

"I don't know."

Mrs. Flanagan hugged me. "We'll keep him for as long as you need."

Mr. Flanagan spoke up. "Take another week off for bereavement leave, but you need to go back to Phim Bros., son. There's work to be done."

"I can't," I said helplessly, spreading my hands. "Impossible."

"Nonsense," he bellowed. "Best way to get over grief is to go on living."

"I don't know how to. I can't imagine going to Phim Bros. every day without my wife in the car, talking my ear off. I don't know how to live like this. I feel like half of my soul has been stolen away."

Mrs. Flanagan patted me on the back. "It's okay, sweetheart." She leaned in and kissed my cheek. I bit back tears; she smelled like Adeline because they used the same perfume. I breathed in slowly. Men didn't cry.

"I'll find something for you," Mr. Flanagan promised. "Something outside of Phim Bros.."

"I'd appreciate that, sir." The

three of us walked back to the car, and everything was quiet as they took me back to the house where my family should be living, a house which was totally empty now, just me rattling around by myself.

When he parked the car in the driveway, he turned around and asked me, "What do you think of San Francisco?"

"San Francisco?"

"There are some exciting new companies out there. I have some friends who are looking to invest in them, but they don't have the time to make the drive. Would you like to be the venture capitalist on the ground, check things out, look at the books, and call back? I can't guarantee anything, but you might be the right man."

San Francisco was a world away from Los Angeles and heartbreak. The empty house. The dead wife.

"I'd take that in a heartbeat, sir."

He nodded. "I'll see what I can do. I'll give you a call next week."

Double Funeral

Allen

TWO YEARS LATER

I was sitting in my office reviewing some ledgers when my secretary knocked on my door.

"I'm busy," I called.

"Sir, you're going to want to take this call. There's been a death in the family." I got to my feet, then I lunged for the receiver.

"Hello?"

"Allen McKane?"

"Yes. Who is this?"

"I'm your nanny, sir."

I was quiet. I'd briefly interviewed her over the phone after she'd gotten Mrs. Flanagan's approval.

"What happened?"

"Mr. and Mrs. Flanagan went out for lunch, but they were hit by a drunk driver. They were pronounced dead on arrival."

"Good Lord."

"Sir, you're going to have to come down and arrange things."

"I'll be there soon." The Flanagans' deaths didn't hit me as hard as Adeline's, and I knew the steps. I'd been through them two years before.

"Can you take care of the baby?"

"Sir, I'm only contracted to take care of the baby from 8 to 5. If you need more than that, you're going to have to hire a night nanny."

I felt like she was speaking another language. "Night nanny?"

"Yes, sir."

I sighed. "Could you give me the

phone number of your agency, please?"

She gave me the phone number, which I scribbled on a sheet of paper.

"Thank you," I told her. "I'll call them right away. Bye."

I hung up the phone before I could say anything else and pinched the bridge of my nose. I could feel the beginning of a tension headache.

I'd sold the first home that Adeline and I had bought together to raise a family in. When I'd made my first million, Mr. Flanagan had given me a gigantic house next to his.

Trevor still lived with the Flanagans,

though I came over for dinner every

weeknight that I was in town to

spend time with the little boy. He was

a cute kid, Adeline's hair and my

eyes, sure, but it felt like he was more

theirs than mine. They'd spent a lot

more time with the baby than I had.

I'd call this nanny agency and

figure things out. I didn't know what

a two-year-old little boy needed. I was

more like a favorite uncle than a

father. I'd never changed any diapers,

and I didn't know the first thing about potty training. Was Trevor housebroken? Was that the word that you used for babies who learned how to use the toilet?

I didn't know jack about Trevor.

* * *

I was bone-tired after the funeral. I'd accepted all the condolences on their behalf. The Flanagans had been well-loved, and I was the only member of the family left besides little Trevor, who stayed at home through the whole thing. A funeral home was no place for a baby. I was really a son-in-law, but the Flanagans had held me close after Adeline's death. They were better parents than mine ever were. All of the warm family time that the Flanagans had encouraged me to have evaporated into thin air now that they were dead, so I was by myself, nannies taking care of my son.

After Adeline's parents died, I realized that the Flanagans' house had to be sold. But then I thought a little more about it, and I decided to sell my own house. Mrs. Flanagan had put a lot of time into her house, while I barely had a mattress on the floor to sleep on. Plus, all of Trevor's stuff was in the other house. I'd just move into their guest room and go from there.

The move-in process was fast. I didn't have much stuff, just some clothes and a little technology. The companies that I invested in gave me prototypes of their stuff when they pitched, and I had a lot of little gizmos.

They were starting to buzz about something that they called the World Wide Web. I didn't know much about it, but all the nerds were very excited about the potential.

I rarely spent nights in Los Angeles anymore. I'd had an apartment in San Francisco, and I had two nannies to take care of the baby. He was totally fine. The Flanagans had willed everything to Trevor with me as the trustee. I'd have control of their fortune until

Trevor reached 30 with a college degree. They weren't young, so they'd put some forethought in how they wanted their money to be distributed when they were gone.

The nannies loved the kid more than I did. Apparently, they had a silly nickname for him. I called to check in once in a while, and the night nanny told me with great pride something that she thought was exciting.

"Trouble slept through the night last night."

"That's great." I slept through the night every night in my cold bed.

"No," she said patiently, as if I had never graduated from grade school. "Babies have to learn how to do that, and he's been restless since his grandparents died."

"I see." I thought back to what she said. "What did you call him? Trouble?"

"Yes. We call this little troublemaker by that name. Trouble," she called. "Come here. I want you to talk to your daddy."

"Da?" I heard a little voice say. "Dada?"

"Yes, Dada." She cleared her throat. "Trouble, can you say your name? Can you tell Daddy your name?"

"Chubba," he told me solemnly. He probably thought that Dada was the word for phone.

"Treh-ver," I said slowly, enunciating clearly. Adeline had chosen his name. It was Irish, and that'd been important to her. She loved her Irish roots. It still hurt to think of her; it felt like someone had stuck a knife in my chest.

The worst part of being a widower with a small child and no support system wasn't the sympathy and the pity in people's eyes. No, the worst part was waking up alone, reaching for a cold pillow because my wife was dead. I wasn't ashamed of crying at those moments, because Adeline's death had left me totally dead inside.

"Chubba," he agreed.

"Trevor."

"Chubba."

"You're not going to win, sir. That's how he says his name now."

I shook my head. "Whatever makes him happy." Trouble wasn't the name that Adeline had chosen, but it'd do.

"When are you coming home, sir?"

"When I'm ready." The home, which had been full of light and warmth when the Flanagans had been alive, was empty now. I had a fortune to make in San Francisco, and Trouble was well taken care of by nannies who loved him. I had nothing to worry about, really, even when one of them went back to school for her master's degree. I just called the nanny agency and replaced them after a quick phone interview.

I wouldn't lie and say that my son was easy to care for. Trouble wasn't a saint by any means. But child care was a problem that could be fixed with money, unlike my broken heart, so I used the copious amount of money that I had to fix it.

Nothing at all could fix my heart.

I tried to date, wanting to get out of the house for more than work, keeping everything in San Francisco. I first found a lady to warm my bed. She was pretty, she was fun, and she wasn't interested in anything serious. We had a pleasant, casual relationship until she moved away.

So I got another. And another after that. And another, until I couldn't keep track anymore.

None of these women were the kind that I'd bring home to meet my son. It turned out that becoming a

billionaire — even just on paper —
made you very handsome. The
dotcom bust hit me hard and pushed
me back down to 9 figures, around
$900,000,000, but I spent the years
after that pushing it back to 10
figures. I belonged in the three
comma club, not the two comma
club, and no temporary setback
would keep me out.

III. Future

Together

Airport

Valentina

SUNDAY AFTERNOON

"Allen, I've got to go."

"You can stay a little while longer. It doesn't take that long to get on a plane."

"Allen, I've got to check my bag and go through security. And I've got to board 30 minutes before takeoff."

"How long does that take?"

"It changes every time. Believe

me, I fly twice a week, if not more. I've got to go now, or I'm going to be late."

Allen frowned at me, naked on my bed. I admired his fit body. It wasn't overly muscular, but he was lean and toned in a way that I really liked. Throughout our dirty weekend, I could not stop myself from tracing the ridges of his six-pack.

"What if I have my jet fly you back to Seattle tonight? Would you stay then?"

"Allen," I said, swallowing hard. "You knew that this was coming. You knew that I was going to leave on Sunday."

"I didn't think that it would come so soon." He got out of bed and began dressing in the clothes that he'd worn to the ball game. He didn't have a phone charger, and I had a Nexus phone, so his iPhone had died sometime that first night. I'd offered to go buy him a new power adapter, but he didn't want me to leave the room. We'd been naked nearly the whole time, making room service leave our food outside of the door and quickly darting outside to get the tray in a bathrobe, hoping no one was there. I'd only just gotten dressed this last time, because I was about to go to the airport.

"I had a really good time with you." I'd packed my bags early this morning, before Allen had woken up. There was an ache in the center of my chest when I thought about leaving him, but this was my job. It's what I did.

"I had a good time with you, too. Sure you don't want to take a jet?"

"I'm sure." I walked to the bed and kissed him lightly. "I'll leave you the key card. You only have to check out by 8 PM tonight. I got an extension."

He grabbed my waist and pulled me a little closer so that I was nearly in his lap. He kissed me hard, and I kissed him back with equal force. It was hard to leave, hard for both of us, I thought.

"If you're ever in LA again..."

"I'll call you." My eyes were filling with tears, so I turned away before he could see it. I was way too emotionally attached to the man who had rocked me up, down, and sideways during this weekend. In the grand scheme of things, the time that we spent together was very short. But I knew that I'd never forget this weekend with this man.

Yeah, he'd blown my mind. He had techniques that I never even heard of. I'd tried more sex positions in the last two days than I'd ever been in before. But he was also kind and caring, funny and sweet despite the past life in a gang.

He'd told me all about his childhood, slinging drugs, stealing cars, all the crimes he'd done. He told me about his wife, Adeline, and how her death had ripped him apart and made him focus completely on business, making him one of the youngest billionaires in North America. I knew that he'd kept all of this inside for a long time, and I'd spent a lot of time listening to him while naked beside him. I got the impression that he needed to let all of it out so that he could move forward.

I knew him well, possibly better than his own kid, the one that he'd basically abandoned at a young age. But I didn't blame him for being hit hard when Adeline suddenly died; my family was tight, but not every family was.

I wiped away my tears discreetly as I grabbed my bag and tote and headed for the door. I felt like my heart was breaking into pieces as I opened the hotel room door for the last time.

Time to face reality. Our magical weekend was over.

Sea-Tac

Valentina

I drove to the airport and returned my rental car. I had TSA Pre-Check, and I went through security without too much trouble. It was nice not to have to remove my shoes. I went and sat in the waiting area before going to the bathroom to cry silently and wipe my tears away. Something inside of me had changed in LA.

Then it was time for me to board my flight. I got into my business class seat and stared out the window. LA was a nice city, and I'd jump at any contracts that brought me back here. Back to Allen.

My flight was taking off. I had a connection at SJC, the airport in San Jose. It was a quick one-hour layover. In the bathroom, there were a ton of signs talking about how they used seawater for waste water, which I thought was interesting. I thought that they had a better solution to

California's extreme drought problem than LAX did, for sure.

It was enough time for me to get off the plane, buy some food, eat it, and then go to my gate. My tears were dry now. I had had a wonderful time, but time was up.

I bought Wi-Fi on the plane ride to Seattle, because I'd neglected my email while I was boning my brains out. I had a bunch of urgent ones, the most recent ones with the red exclamation that noted a very urgent email in Outlook.

Joy.

But I couldn't ignore my responsibilities forever. I sent them all off, replying to everyone and talking about everything that had fallen apart over the course of the weekend. I was a consultant, but I also did a lot of internal work on certain task forces. My consulting company was always talking about improvement, liking the Toyota method of kaizen, and I was in charge of some of our international efforts since I spoke Spanish.

I heard the pilot telling me to stow all electronics, then we were landing. I had the information for my hotel. I got off the plane with my tote bag and went to wait at the carousel for my baggage.

I could see a lot of men in suits holding boards with names on them. I went to look for which carousel I should be getting my bag at. According to the computer screens, number fourteen was the right one.

When I walked over to number fourteen, there was a man there who had on sunglasses and a chauffeur's hat. I did a double take when I realized that my name was on the board.

"Dr. Valentina Baez?"

"Just Valentina. What are you...?"

And then he took the sunglasses off, and I realized that it was Allen.

Before I knew what I was doing, I was throwing myself at him. He caught me in his arms and kissed me fiercely.

"Did you really think that I'd let

you go that easily?" he whispered in my ear before biting it. "You make me feel alive, and that's too precious to just let you walk away."

"How did you even get here?"

"I took my jet."

"Your jet. Of course," I laughed before kissing him again.

"But wait a minute...you have a business."

"I can do a lot of things remotely. They're used to me being in San Francisco and Singapore. As long as you can leave me alone during the normal workday, I'll be fine."

"I can safely promise you that." I got to the hospital at 7 and left at 7, just like a nurse, so it wouldn't be an issue. But we'd talk about our schedules later.

I didn't have to rent a car, it turned out. Allen had commissioned a chauffeur for the week, and we were traveling in style in a big black SUV. I looked outside.

"Isn't Mount Rainier near Seattle?"

"You can't see it right now

because of the clouds, miss," our
driver told me.

"Oh," I replied. "Thanks."

Allen's hand was on my knee
now. He squeezed me gently. I put my
hand on his. I was so glad that he'd
come for me. We'd figure something
out.

Barfing

Valentina

THREE MONTHS LATER

Allen and I had figured out a way to accommodate each other's schedules over the course of the three months after he followed me to Seattle. I only worked four days a week, so we went to LA for Friday, Saturday, and Sunday. He had meetings on Saturday, but he said that it was worth it. I knew that he shouldn't be gone right then, not with the impending hostile takeover of Star and possible reverse takeover of Majuscule, but he said that I was worth it. He was willing to lose his billionaire status just for me.

Allen had to go back to LA for some meetings with the board of Star, so I was on my own for two days before I flew down to LA. I had to admit that having a chartered jet was a lot more fun and convenient than using normal commercial flights. Allen let me use the plane in any way that I wanted — including getting sweaty in the small bedroom in the back of some of the jets. Traveling twice a week was now a pleasure with Allen always by my side.

Everything was smooth sailing until I started barfing during a breakfast meeting in Denver. The scent of bacon and coffee sent me to the trash can with no time to run to the bathroom. They smelled utterly vile to me, which was crazy. I was the kind of girl who liked to indulge sometimes with an egg, bacon, and cheese sandwich with a white chocolate mocha latte.

But there I was, barfing everything that I'd just eaten for breakfast into the trash can.

When I was finally done, my hands were shaking. The illness didn't make me tremble; the thought of what it meant was hitting me. The meeting room was full of people who were staring at me.

"Excuse me," I said, wiping my mouth with the back of my hand and tasting the disgusting taste of vomit.

"I've got to go."

I grabbed my briefcase and went to the bathroom so that I could rinse out my mouth. After I spat out some water, I popped a mint to take away some of the taste. I knew where I needed to go now: a pharmacy.

I was in a hospital, but I'd avoid going to a doctor when pregnancy could be assessed with a simple at-home test. I went to the pharmacy downstairs that was part of the gift shop. It had things like sugar-free candy for diabetics and a bunch of simple OTC medicines, like cough drops.

They only had two brands of pregnancy tests in there, but I brought them to the register.

"Are you expecting?"

"I don't know," I said. I watched her look at my bare hands. No rings. I could feel her silently judging me, but she said nothing more.

I handed her my card so that I could get out of there. She swiped it, I signed the receipt, and then I took the bag that she offered me. I needed to get back to my hotel room as soon

as I could.

Pregnancy Test

Valentina

My hands were shaking even more than before as I swiped my card. It took me two tries to open the door, because I missed the slot the first time.

And then I was inside with a small bag that had two tests that could change my life forever.

I went to the bathroom and read the instructions on the back. If there

were two lines, then I'd have a baby.
One line, and I was safe.

I realized that we'd never used
protection. I felt like throwing up
again. None of this was planned. We'd
been together for three months, but
we were enjoying each other's
company. It wasn't like he was going
to get down on his knee and make me
Mrs. Billionaire tomorrow.

Marriage wasn't something I
planned on anytime soon.. I had my
PhD; I meant to go places, to have a
solid career already set up before

settling down and having kids. And all of that was left in the dust because I hadn't thought to ask him to use condoms or to go to the doctor for birth control after the long drought that I'd had.

I walked into the bathroom. I looked at the mirror. My face was a little paler than usual. The harsh light of the bathroom made me look exhausted.

And terrified.

Pretty accurate. I worked twelve hours a day on site and more at night in my hotel room, though that was more pleasurable since Allen and I tended to work at night while in bed together. Naked.

We might have made a baby during one of those nights together. I went to the toilet and peed on the first stick. Then I peed on the second one. I wiped myself, pulled up my panties, and washed my hands. I needed to wait for a little while.

I went to my bed and flopped onto it. I stared at the pure white ceiling. How would my life change if I had a baby?

If I was pregnant, should I abort it? The baby wasn't planned, and I was scared of how it could shake Allen up. I didn't think that he was going to try to have a kid now. Laila, his daughter-in-law, was pregnant at the moment. How would it feel to have a child who was younger than his own grandson? Would he just walk away and never look back?

I felt my breathing start to speed up, just under a rate that I would consider hyperventilating. Tears were threatening, sitting at the corners of my eyes. I blinked once and they fell down my temples and went into my ears. I was too miserable to sit up. A baby would ruin everything that I'd worked for. It would ruin my relationship with Allen.

My phone rang. I ignored it. I couldn't deal with anybody right now.

Finally, it was time for me to check the pregnancy tests. I already knew the answer when I went into the bathroom.

Two tests, both with two lines.

I touched my stomach. It felt the same as ever, but everything had changed.

I had a baby in there now.

Takeover

Allen

The day after I finally completed the acquisition of Majuscule, I was in a meeting with Mateo, the man who'd made the whole thing happen, the man who had targeted Star.

"I'll fucking kill you." The man across the table from me banged his fist against the table, making the solid maple shake. "How dare you acquire Majuscule? How did you even get the money?" Mateo's face was as red as a tomato.

I shrugged. "This is the game. Thanks for playing."

"You fucking asshole!" He tried to lunge across the table, but his lawyer held the back of his suit jacket.

I didn't move an inch. I'd grown up on the streets of LA. I didn't have anything to fear from this Harvard-educated buffoon. I could kick his ass twice and not even sweat.

"Don't," his lawyer told him.

"I will fucking ruin you," he told

me. "I will take everything you hold dear. I will ruin your life just like you ruined mine."

"Don't let the door hit you on the way out."

He stormed towards the door with his lawyer right behind him. The door hit the wall with enough force to make the entire room shake, which was surprising, since everything in California was built to withstand earthquakes.

"You shouldn't have provoked him like that," my lawyer told me mildly. "You shouldn't be a sore winner."

I leaned forward. "Are you fucking joking? He tried to come for me. I don't come to play. He's lucky that his job is the only thing that he lost. I could've targeted his wife, his kids, his bank accounts...his security is pretty appalling."

"It's not a smart idea to antagonize someone who has lost everything, Allen."

I shrugged. "I can take him any day."

"What if he targets someone who isn't you?"

"Trouble? He can take care of himself." He understood the security risks associated with being in our position; he knew what to do.

"Is there anybody else who matters to you?"

I thought for only half a second before a cold shiver passed through my body.

"Valentina."

"You better increase her security for the next few months."

"I will. I've got to go."

I grabbed my briefcase and ran out of the meeting room to get to my car. I dialed Ellie so that I could put my phone on speakerphone while I drove to the airfield.

"Ellie," I said without any greeting, "I need you to call JetSuite and get a jet to go to Seattle immediately. I also need you to get a security detail for Valentina in Seattle, one that will move with us. We've got to move right now."

I called Valentina, but she didn't

answer her phone. She was probably just busy. Or something.

I leaned back and thought of someone stealing her — kidnapping my girlfriend. My lover. He'd seen this coming for a couple months. He could already have a team in place.

I clenched my fist. While I was in the jet, I was helpless. I couldn't help her in LA. I'd go to her as fast as I could, but I could already be too late.

Almost Stolen

Valentina

There was a sharp knock on the door. I quickly threw the pregnancy tests in the trash. I'd deal with them later. I smoothed my hair before I went to the door.

Outside were two men in the security uniforms of the hotel. Its name was embossed on their right-hand shirt pockets.

"Valentina Baez?"

"That's me. How can I help you?"

"We were sent by Allen McKane. We need to take you somewhere safe."

"What are you talking about?" I frowned. Allen hadn't talked to me since our nightly phone call right before bed last night. "Let me check my phone."

I turned away from the door, but one of the security guards pushed it open.

"We don't have time for that. We've got to go."

The two of them got behind me and started pushing me towards the staircase.

"Why aren't we taking the elevators? Where are you taking me?"

"There will be time for questions later, ma'am." They kept hustling me down the stairs, so fast that I nearly tripped and had to catch myself on the rail. What if I fell on the concrete stairs? The baby would be hurt.

"You have to slow down. I can't move this fast."

One of them picked me up and

slung me over his shoulder.

"Hey! Put me down!"

"We don't have time for this."

I beat on his back, but he didn't do anything. He wasn't even breathing hard as he ran down the stairs. The other guard was running even faster. They had a security van waiting outside. The other guard went to the driver's side. The one holding me got into the back.

"What's happening?"

The engine started.

"Where are we going?"

Right then, I heard the wail of police sirens.

"Motherfucker," one of the guards said.

"What's going on?" I could hear the edge of hysteria in my voice. I was still upset from learning that I was pregnant, and now I was in a van with two men who said that Allen had sent them.

There was a police car at the entrance of the parking lot now. Allen was getting out of the car.

"Run," the first guard said to the

other. They got out of the car and ran for it.

I ran to Allen.

"What's going on?"

"Are you hurt?"

"No."

He touched me gently all over my body, not in a sexual way at all. He seemed to be looking for bruises or some evidence of manhandling, but I was just fine.

"Allen, what just happened?"

He sighed. "You know about the Majuscule situation?"

"Yes."

"The main partner who was engineering the Star hostile takeover lost his job, and he swore to get revenge on me. I've got a solid security team. So does Trouble, though he mostly ignores them. The only element that isn't locked down is…"

"Me." I nodded. "I don't move around with a security team."

"Yeah, that's about to change. You're not going anywhere without security from now on."

"Allen," I protested, "I have a job."

"You can do your job with security."

"Allen, that's crazy."

"I'd do anything to keep you safe." I could hear just a hint of desperation in his voice. I thought about what would have happened if they'd successfully kidnapped me, and I understood why he wanted to have security. "Can you get off of work early this week?"

"Yes. I just about wrapped everything up early, so I can go home now. They think that I'm sick, anyway. I barfed today."

"Do you need to see a doctor?"

I didn't want to see a doctor, though I knew that inevitably I would have to go to one.

"No."

"Get into the police car. He'll take us to the airfield. I've got a charter going somewhere safe. We're going to file the flight plan at the last minute so that they can't trace us."

"Where are we going?"

"Into the car."

I followed him more willingly than I had followed those fake security guards wearing hotel uniforms. I knew that he was acting in my best interests.

The cop drove us to the airfield.

"Thank you for coming and saving me," I told him. Sergeant Nguyen, his uniform said.

"My job, ma'am." He nodded at me and then Allen.

"Let's go." Allen was climbing the steps into the aircraft now, so I followed him.

Secret Island

Valentina

When we got into the plane, I instantly saw that this plane ride wouldn't be like our other ones. For one thing, the jet was packed with huge guys, the kind of guys that you'd cross the street to avoid. Oh, they were all clean and clean-shaven. But they all had huge muscles, and a few of them had tattoos like Allen's. Only they were younger and had something hard in their eyes.

"Who are these people?"

"I needed to get security people immediately, so I pulled on some of my own contacts. I didn't want to go with a normal security firm. I tend to use one, and he could have found out."

"Who?"

"The partner at Majuscule, Mateo."

I nodded. "Okay."

I buckled in. Allen was in the seat next to me. He reached for my hand and laced our fingers together. His pulse was coming in fast. Seeing me almost kidnapped had definitely messed with him, and he didn't even know about the baby yet.

I bit my lip. This wasn't the right time to tell him about the baby. We weren't in private. We were in a plane full of strangers.

I rested my head on his broad shoulder.

"Sleep, babe." His hand came up to stroke my hair.

I felt really jittery, but I was also

tired out by the events of the day.

As we took off, the rumble of the engines lulled me to sleep.

* * *

When I woke up, we were landing.

"Where are we?"

"An island."

I looked out the window. I could see a long expanse of green-turquoise water and white sand on the beach. The island was pretty small. I could see all the way around it, and we weren't even that high.

"What island is this?"

"I bought it."

"I beg your pardon?"

"I bought it for you."

I didn't even know how to respond to that declaration.

One, he bought an island. Two, it was for me.

"That's...interesting."

"I need to keep you safe."

"I work, you know."

"You don't have to."

"Yes, I do."

"You don't. I can take care of

you."

I snorted. "I'd never rely on a man for money. Not ever. Not even you, Allen."

"How about I hire you? You can work for me."

"Same thing in a different package."

"You can't take any more contracts right now. Do you know what it was like when I saw you in that van?"

I was quiet. I knew what he must have thought.

"We'll discuss it later."

We felt the jolt of the plane finally landing on the island that Allen had bought for me. I put my hand on my stomach. I'd thought about aborting the child, but now I was pretty sure that I didn't want to kill my baby; I'd been scared on those stairs that something would hurt the baby and induce a miscarriage. I'd figure out a way forward for the baby. The idea of the security guards hurting my baby hurt me, and I knew that I'd never be able to kill my baby just because he or she was unplanned.

The plane taxied to a stop.

"Let's go." Allen unlatched the cabin door, which slowly extended downwards. His hand was in mine.

"All of my stuff is in that hotel in Denver."

"I can send someone to get it. I'm tightly controlling everything coming in and out of this island. The boat dock has a million cameras on it. The airfield has motion sensors that are so sensitive that they detect rain. I'm leaving nothing to chance."

"Why is all of this necessary?"

"I put Ellie on it. Apparently, Mateo somehow knew Gino."

"Who is Gino?"

"Ambrogino Moretti, the former gang leader of my gang back in the day."

"What?"

"What you need to know is that Gino just got out of prison."

"And why does that matter for us?"

"Gino hates me."

"Why?"

"He blames me for the manslaughter conviction that he got. It's not my fault that he had an itchy trigger finger."

"He killed someone?"

Allen shuffled his feet. "We were stealing a car. Someone came by. Gino just shot before thinking. He's been in prison for more than twenty years now. Ellie says that he's some sort of crime lord. He has a network of prisoners that reaches throughout the entire California penitentiary system."

"Crime lord?"

"He runs a shadow organization, and he's ready to come for me. Mateo hit the right buttons. He found Gino with only a little digging. This takeover has been going on for months. They've had time to plan what they would do if I won."

"Kidnap me?"

"Yes."

My heart beat fast when I thought about being captured by people who hated Allen. It wouldn't be good for me, and it would be even worse for my baby...the baby that Allen still didn't know about.

"So where are we going to stay?"

"There's a large mansion here. Our guards will stay in the guardhouse."

There were black SUVs waiting at the edge of the airfield, and Allen and I climbed into one. The island wasn't very big, and it was just a few minutes before I saw an enormous white mansion on a low hill.

"Holy cow. That's big."

"It's just enough."

"There are only two of us."

Allen shrugged. "It's not like I'd be able to find a shack with the kind of security that I wanted for you."

I put a hand on my stomach. This house was good enough for the baby. I didn't want the baby to be protected in a shack, either.

"Believe me, that house has a lot better security than a shack. The advance team vetted it very thoroughly. It's almost impossible to get in or off this island." Our driver was speaking.

"Thank you...what's your name?"

"Severin, ma'am." I could see the flash of his white teeth in the rearview mirror. He was a handsome guy.

"Thank you, Severin."

Allen pulled my hand into his. I leaned against him, taking strength from his solid body and his dark, masculine scent. We'd make it through this somehow.

Chocolate Gelato

Valentina

When we got to the house, Allen was off to check every corner of it.

Severin helped me get out of the SUV. There was a running board, but he just lifted me gently out of it to put me on the ground.

"Thank you, Severin."

"Do you have any luggage?"

"None." After that attempted kidnapping, I didn't have a thing with me. I hoped that Allen would send someone for my stuff soon. If we didn't mind alerting my parents that someone had tried to kidnap me, I could even ask my mom to mail me stuff. I didn't want to concern her unnecessarily, though. She was a little flighty, and the thought of her baby girl being kidnapped would end in someone getting hurt.

"How does ice cream sound?"

My head snapped around as I looked at him. "What?" Food was the last thing on my mind.

"Ice cream. Do you want some?"

"Um, yes."

"Then come to the kitchen."

We went into the kitchen, where he opened the freezer.

"The advance team came here a few hours before the rest of you. He mobilized people from the mainland to come here. I had the time to make some gelato."

"You know how to make gelato?" I looked him up and down. He looked like the kind of guy who ate raw steak for breakfast.

"My grandmother taught me."

I hoped that it was good. "Sounds cool." My mother taught me everything that I ever needed to know about pie, but beyond that, I couldn't cook, mostly bake.

He pulled a metal canister out of the freezer and opened a drawer to bring out an ice cream scoop, then he put gelato into two bowls.

"Mmm, this is really good. Chocolate?"

"Chocolate hazelnut."

"Even better." I finished my bowl.

Without a word, he put all the rest of the gelato in it.

"Thank you, Severin."

He shrugged. "There's not enough for everyone. We should finish it before they figure it out." He winked at me, and my cheeks warmed. I was here with my billionaire lover, but I thought that Severin was flirting with me.

Allen came into the kitchen then.

"I heard voices."

"I was just eating some chocolate ice cream."

"What? Weren't you just barfing?"

"I'm much better now." Did Allen not know that ice cream could solve a lot of problems, if only temporarily? Ice cream was a Band-Aid that didn't address the root cause, but treating the symptom was pretty great.

"There's chocolate at the corner of your mouth," Allen said, bending down to kiss me and licking it off of me. "Mm."

Because Severin was sitting right there, I blushed, thinking about how this must look.

"Let's go upstairs."

Allen pulled my hand.

"Thanks, Severin," I said for the last time before Allen pulled me away.

Baby Trap

Valentina

My suitcase arrived the next day in the jet. Allen and I spent all of our time in the house. It wasn't like the time that we had spent together in hotels. He was obsessed with looking at the monitors that showed the feeds from all of the security cameras covering the entire house.

I was grateful to get my suitcase and laptop. At least with the laptop I had something to do all day.

Allen's mansion didn't have Wi-Fi. It wasn't like they ran fiber optic cables out here. But I had a little USB dongle that could connect to the Internet wherever it was, so I was fine. I wouldn't be able to watch a ton of music videos or something, but I could function at least.

First of all, I sent off an email to my supervisor at the consulting company. My bosses changed every week, but the head of practice was my actual boss. I told her that I'd be out of commission for a while. I briefly described the attempted kidnapping and the situation at hand.

I soon got an email back telling me not to worry and that they'd take care of everything. I breathed a sigh of relief. I was the only one on the team who did certain things, but I was glad to see that they'd function without me.

"What are you doing?" Allen had walked back into the room.

"I'm just emailing my boss."

"Why are you working?"

"It's courteous and professional."

Allen nodded. "Yes. What did you say?"

"I told her about the kidnapping. She already heard about me barfing from the team in the meeting where I did it."

Allen frowned. "I meant to ask you about that, but I got distracted. Why were you barfing? Do I need to buy Gatorade and some soda to help settle your stomach?"

I shook my head. "Soda would

probably help, but I don't think that Gatorade would really help."

"Why?"

I took a deep breath. "I don't have a stomach bug."

"What do you mean?"

I spelled it out with two words. "I'm pregnant."

You could've heard a pin drop in that room.

"What?"

"I'm pregnant," I repeated. "It's your baby."

"You're aborting it." It wasn't a

question. It was a statement.

"No, I'm not."

"I never pegged you as a golddigger."

I crossed my arms across my chest. "I'm not a golddigger."

"How did this happen?"

"We never used protection."

"Aren't you on the pill?"

"No. Before I was with you, I was abstinent for a long time."

"I never thought to ask. I just assumed that all sexually active women used it."

I shrugged. "This sexually active woman did not use it."

"If you want to keep me, you'll abort the baby."

My jaw dropped until it almost touched the ground.

"What?"

"I want to make sure that you're not doing this because you think that it'll set you up for life."

"I'm not! Are you joking?"

"You're not the only woman to try to snare me with a baby trap."

"I'm never aborting this child."

"Then we're done." He spun and walked out of the room.

Breakup

Valentina

I stared at the open doorway. I could not believe that he'd reacted like that. I felt ashamed of all of the dreams that I'd had when I first decided to keep the baby. Tears filled my eyes. How could he do this to me?

I knew that he was way beyond my level, but I thought that we had something real...an honest connection. He said that he liked me.

I knew that I loved him.

It was obvious that love wasn't enough...one-sided love anyway. I put my hand on my stomach, thinking about the little person who was growing inside of me. Tears were dripping down my cheeks now, and I knew that I was an ugly crier.

I went to the nightstand to grab the tissue box. I knew that I was going to need it.

At the chair by the window, I looked outside at the storm that had just started. I'd always liked watching the lightning when I was a little kid, and it felt like the thunderstorm understood how I felt right now.

I loved him — I knew that — and no words could change that. But I also understood that I could not shape the world according to my desires. Just loving him didn't mean that he had to love me back. He obviously didn't want the baby, so what were my options?

I had enough money to keep us afloat for a little while, as long as there weren't complications with the birth.

"I'll love you," I swore to my baby, nestled safely inside of me. "I'll love you enough for two parents, I promise."

My breaths were slowing down now, and my tears slowed. I knew that I had done the right thing when I told him, but I hadn't expected him to demand an abortion. My child was the most important thing in the world to me now — the most important thing in the world to me ever — and I knew that I needed to figure out a way to get off of this island.

I went to the closet and wiped my tears. I needed to focus on packing. All of the stuff that I'd put up on hangers was thrown into my suitcase, no careful packing. When I went on airplane trips, I tried to maximize the space to fit way too many clothes inside. This time, I just shoved an enormous heap inside and forced the suitcase shut. I needed to get out of here, far away from Allen.

I went to the bathroom to splash water on my face so that I could hide my red eyes. I didn't want to scare anybody away by looking like a demon. It was better to be like this. I wished that I had some eye drops, but I hadn't packed my own stuff when we came to this island. It was in a first-aid kit at home.

I blew out a long breath and looked into the mirror. I was sure of my path now. I'd get off this island, go home, forget that I ever heard of Allen McKane, and raise my baby by myself. I'd be the best mother a baby could ever ask for; it didn't matter that his or her dad wanted nothing to do with him or her. The baby would always know that he or she was loved, no matter what.

I dragged the suitcase down the stairs, then I headed for the guardhouse. I found the right door, and I knocked.

Severin

Valentina

"Severin?"

The door opened, and I saw that Severin was half-dressed, shirtless. He had a lot of scars. He frowned at me and looked at my suitcase.

"What's going on?"

"Can you take me home, please? The plane is the best way off of the island." I hated how pathetic my voice sounded when it cracked at the end of that sentence. I slung one arm across my vulnerable stomach. I knew that he could clearly see what happened, and I saw a flash of pity in his eyes.

"Of course I can get the plane. Let me grab a co-pilot, and we'll take you away from the island. Wait here, okay?" He opened the door a little wider. "It's a mess, but it'll have to do."

I looked around his room. To be honest, it looked a lot like what my room at home looked like:

comfortable and lived in.

"Okay."

I sat in the chair by his desk as I waited for him to come back with someone else. There were a lot of papers in Italian on his desk that I couldn't read. I had never learned Italian, so I couldn't even begin to guess what the papers said.

Someone rapped on the door. I looked up. They were standing there, Severin and Sergio, and they were ready to go. Both of them had on leather jackets. For the first time, they actually looked like dangerous guards. When I had met them, they'd looked like college students on a vacation. Now they looked like the bodyguards that they were. I felt instantly safer with the two of them.

Severin picked up my suitcase and held it.

"Let's go."

The three of us walked quickly to the runway, not too far from the guardhouse. Sergio kept looking over his shoulder; I wanted to tell him not to even bother. Allen wasn't going to look for me. We were done.

The three of us walked to the plane and walked inside. I could tell that the two of them were used to working together, because they instantly snapped to a bunch of different tasks. I'd seen a clipboard and physical checklist that pilots used when they flew, but Severin and Sergio seemed to have the list memorized.

I shivered in the cool night air.

"We'll be home soon, baby," I whispered to my stomach. "Nobody will hurt us there." So what if Allen had only hurt me emotionally? I felt like crumpling into a ball and licking my wounds. I wouldn't be ready to see him anytime soon, though I guessed that he would want to see me after the baby was born to make arrangements.

"Nobody will make me give you up," I promised my baby. "Nobody can ever do that."

I heard the engines turn on, and I fastened my seatbelt a half second before Severin told me, "Buckle up."

I felt the plane move beneath me as we sped up faster and faster. Suddenly, one of the pilots slammed on the brakes. When I looked forward towards the cockpit, I could see that there was a car on the runway.

Running

Allen

When I got back to the house after clearing my head, I walked up to our bedroom. I wanted to change out of clothes that weren't sweaty from the humidity. I needed to talk to Valentina. After seeing that half of the closet was empty, I realized that Valentina had packed. Tension nestled between my shoulder blades. I had to go find her and apologize before she decided that I wasn't worth the pain.

Guilt twisted in my gut when I thought of my instinctive reaction. I had been wrong to suggest that she have an abortion; I would make it up to her when I found her. I hurried downstairs to go through the house, but she wasn't anywhere.

That was strange. I briskly walked to the guardhouse and knocked on the door.

Anthony opened it.

"Yeah, boss?"

"I'm looking for Valentina. Have you seen her?"

"She came by fifteen or thirty minutes ago. I think she went to talk to Severin. You can check his room yourself." He pointed.

Anthony backed up as I walked to Severin's room. Nobody was there.

On the desk were papers. I glanced down at them, not really wanting to pry into Severin's private affairs, but then I read them.

Oh, shit.

Severin was a hitman for Gino's

shadow organization. The papers said in plain Italian what his orders were: get close to Valentina, abduct her, and then murder her on video so that Gino could send a video to me and take control of Star in the confusion of the aftermath.

I was grateful that Gino didn't know about the baby, but I also didn't know if that would make the situation better or worse. Gino was obviously trying to mess with me; he knew about the funk that I'd been in after Adeline had died.

I wasn't going to lose two women in one lifetime. One was more than enough. I needed to save Valentina from the men that both of us had trusted.

I went running through the doorway, shouting for the guards to come to the runway. After a beat of silence, all of them started grabbing their guns.

"I want to get in a car."

Anthony grabbed car keys, and the two of us ran to the nearest SUV and gunned for the airfield. I prayed that we wouldn't be too late to get Valentina and my child safely out of the plane.

It was funny, because when Valentina had told me only a little while ago that she was expecting a kid, I didn't want it. But now that she was in danger and the baby's life was at risk, I realized how precious that little person was. I needed to save them both.

Anthony was driving at a speed which, back on the mainland, would get us pulled over by cops, but I still wished that he would go faster.

Then we were crashing through the gate to the airfield. I could see the propellers whirling as the plane started up. My mouth felt dry, and my heart was beating very quickly.

Was I going to be too late?

Car

Valentina

"Who the hell is that?"

Sergio squinted through the windshield. "Looks like Anthony."

"What the fuck is he doing on the runway?"

"He's not alone. Motherfucker!" Sergio's fists slapped the control panel. "I think it's McKane."

"Fuck me," Severin breathed. "So close. Guess we're going to have to go with Plan B."

"What's Plan B?" I asked.

"Shh," Severin said. "We've got to time this right. Okay, here's what we're going to do. We're going to drive the plane to the edge of the airfield and try to get away from the car. We might also try to get off the ground bouncing on the grass, but that's pretty risky. If we run into the woods, we're going to need you to be ready to run, okay?"

I nodded. "Okay." I'd do anything to avoid talking to Allen at the moment. I wasn't a strong runner, but I'd be able to run if they needed me to.

The plane spun sharply around as we aimed for the edge of the fence. The car followed us, and it became abundantly clear that we were not going to be able to make it into the air.

"In five seconds, we're going to run, okay?" The plane came to a shuddering halt. Severin ran for the opening and unlatched it.

"Go!"

He pushed me out a little too roughly, and I didn't land on my feet outside. I was on my hands and knees with e bits of gravel in my palms; I was lightly bleeding. But I didn't have time to care about it now. We needed to move, no matter how much my knees hurt.

We ran into the forest. They'd be able to follow us on foot, but there wasn't anything on the island that could pursue us through the dense forest.

I had exercise asthma, and my

breathing became labored as we went onwards. Finally, I reached the point where I told Severin, "I can't run anymore."

He slapped me across the face. "Run."

I stared at him stupidly, not understanding why he was hurting me. "What?"

He slapped me again. "Run, you stupid bitch."

"Hell no! Don't you dare..."

He punched me in the gut this time, and I put my hands over my stomach. What if he had hurt the baby? His hand came to grip my wrist tightly, so tightly that it would definitely bruise, then he dragged me beside and behind him as Sergio led the three of us towards some rocks.

"What the hell!" I screeched as I panted, my chest heaving. "What the fuck do you think that you're doing?"

"What does it look like?" Severin sneered. "We're taking you away from the island. We've had a boat stashed here since we came, and it's a good thing, too. We're going to have to use it to get away from your fucking lover."

I blinked. "What on earth is happening?"

"Damn, you are one stupid bitch. You're being kidnapped. I have to wait to kill you until I have a videocamera, but trust me, I'm going to enjoy every minute of it."

I pulled away in earnest now, but he was much stronger than me. I thought that he enjoyed it when I tried to get away. My wrist ached like it might be sprained or even broken now by the force with which he was holding me while I struggled.

"Too late, you idiot," he laughed. "You ran straight towards us."

"Help!" I screamed. "Somebody, help!"

I was backhanded again; this time, the blow was so hard that it sent me sprawling on the ground, his hand still holding my wrist. "You really are a stupid bitch, aren't you? There's nobody here but us. In a minute, we'll be on a boat and you'll never see McKane again."

Boat

Allen

I ran through the forest as quietly as I could, remembering from my wilderness survival course that I needed to hold myself differently in order to run silently.

I followed them as they crashed through the forest. There was a guard with me trying not to make noise, but I winced every time that a twig snapped under his foot. I would pay for all of my security guards to go through wilderness training if I got out of this thing alive.

We finally got near a small rocky beach. I had tight controls on the only dock on the island, but there was obviously a security hole here. If you approached this beach in the right way, you could land. There was a boat moored there, tied to a red mangrove that went into the water. I'd fix it if I made it out of this alive.

I reached for the gun that I didn't have. Right. After reading the papers that Severin had left on his desk, I had been so filled with panic that I'd forgotten to get one.

I kept a pocket knife in my pants pocket, but it had been a long time since I'd carried a switchblade. Guys in my gang carried concealed weapons without permits; it was how you stayed alive. I felt like my instincts were rusty, perhaps enough to get me killed.

Anthony had a gun, though, and now that we weren't running anymore, he was quiet. We watched as they slapped Valentina around. Anthony held me back when I would've run there to stop them and kill them.

"We need to wait. The others will come soon. It's two guns against one right now."

"I can't watch this." I saw Valentina hit the ground from the force of Severin's blow. I lunged forward, intent on bashing their heads in.

"Don't," Anthony told me. "Turn towards the tree." His hand was on my wrist.

He pulled me and spun me towards the tree, which was a mistake on his part. Spinning, I deftly grabbed his gun and went running towards Valentina, yanking my wrist away from Anthony fast enough for him to be caught off guard.

Sergio saw me first. "McKane?"

Severin spun around and looked at me. When he saw me, he smiled. His gun was in his hand now, and it was pressed to Valentina's head.

"Valentina!"

"Allen," she whispered. She was crying now, breath coming in hard sobs.

"Put down your gun or the bitch gets it. I have to admit, McKane, I'm a little disappointed that this is happening without a videocamera. But my boss will pay me half of my bonus if I dispose of her, and I think that this is the perfect time, don't you?"

I heard the click as he pulled back the safety on his gun.

"Nice and easy. Do it real slow

now. You wouldn't want me to get startled, not with my gun to Valentina's head, right?"

I slowly knelt and put my gun on the ground. Sergio came over to grab it. When he had it in his hand with the safety on, he kicked me in the head.

The blow was dizzying, and another one came. It felt worse than it should have, because I knew that I had failed Valentina and the baby that she held inside of her.

Sergio grabbed my wrists and

pulled them behind me, securing me with the zip-ties that he had in a pocket. He pushed me until I was in the boat that they had waiting. They put me on a bench next to Valentina. I couldn't put my arms around her, but I rested my leg against hers so that she'd know that I was there. I couldn't do much with my hands literally zip-tied together, but I had watched videos on Youtube of how to get out of zip-ties. I just had to do it discreetly enough for them not to notice.

Zip-ties were made out of plastic; as long as you pulled them enough, they would give like plastic. I pulled and strained against them as quietly and unobtrusively as I could.

I could feel Valentina's entire body shaking next to mine, and her breaths were coming in rapid gasps. She was scared, I knew, and I couldn't tell her that we'd be free in a matter of minutes.

Overboard

Allen

Severin and Sergio didn't seem to be very well-versed in how to use a boat, because it took them a long time to figure out how to start the motor. I guessed that their plan hadn't taken into account how infrequently they'd used a boat.

"I think this fucking motor is broken."

"Piece of shit." Severin kicked the

motor. "We're going to have to row."

Sergio looked at Valentina, then he looked at me. "Can we make them row?"

"No. That's a dumbass idea. These paddles can be used as weapons. We'd shoot them first, but they could knock us out with these things."

I looked at the paddles. Severin was right; they could be used as weapons. Hope swelled in my chest. I wasn't an accomplished seaman, but it didn't take a genius to figure out how to use a blunt weapon for defense purposes. Plenty of people kept baseball bats by their beds for this exact use.

I had finally worked my wrists out of the zip-ties, and I made sure that the one on my right wrist dropped without a sound on the bench behind me. Valentina was still tied. I wouldn't leave without her. I had to figure out how to get both of us off of this boat.

Anthony was still on the mainland, unarmed and probably

pissed that I'd jumped the gun and probably gotten a concussion.

Finally, they untied the boat from the tree and pushed off.

"These oars are the fucking worst. My back is already killing me."

"Shut it," Severin told Sergio. "We have to get out of here before the others arrive."

Sergio and Severin rowed for another minute, Sergio still cursing under his breath. His lack of skill with the oars was going to be my opening.

We were slowly getting into deeper water now, and I knew that my plan wouldn't work if we were too deep.

I turned to Valentina.

"Take a deep breath."

"What?"

"Now."

She took a deep breath. I grabbed the back of her shirt and dove into the water. She struggled against me, but I made both of us sink.

People hold more oxygen inside of them than they think. It's possible for a normal human being to go without breath for about a minute without passing out, as long as you don't hit your head or do anything stupid. It defies our natural instincts to hold our breaths, though, and few people would ever find out empirically how long it would take for them to black out.

I wasn't as strong of a swimmer as my son, but I'd learned how to swim when I was a young kid. My teacher said that I was a fish. Swimming was like riding a bicycle;

somehow, my legs and arms knew exactly what to do to save our three lives.

I found the ground and stood on it, still crouching beneath the water. I could hear the muffled thumps of gunfire, and I hoped that they had exhausted their magazines when they shot at us.

Water resistance is an interesting thing. If you move slowly through water, it doesn't resist very much. But when you move at high velocity through water, it will slow you down considerably. Water behaves not unlike concrete when hit by a bullet. I was glad that the water was warm enough that we wouldn't die of hypothermia rather than asphyxiation.

Valentina had stopped struggling, but I looked at her face. She was just about to the point that she'd breathe in water, which was never a good thing. I pulled her as I walked up the slight gradient to get where she could stand, too. She was almost a foot shorter than me, so I was going to have to hold her up. I hoped that her petite stature wasn't going to be the death of both of us.

As we got closer to the shore, there were tons of roots. That's right; the red mangroves grew directly in the water, which was why they were so effective as fish nurseries. I dodged quickly under the cover of the mangrove roots,; not sufficient cover — I'd prefer Kevlar over a couple of roots any day — but it was going to have to be enough.

I pushed Valentina up, and I felt

her cough out a little seawater as she took in gasping breaths. I let her down, then I went up for a breath, too.

I watched as my guards fired on the two in the boat. Sergio and Severin were out of ammunition and rowing for their lives, but they weren't faster than the bullets. The guards had a small inflatable raft in the back of one of the golf carts that they had taken all the way around the island to get to this cove. I realized that Anthony had one of the radios with him, which meant that they knew where to find us.

We were going to be okay. I pulled at the zip-ties on Valentina's wrists. We'd be able to cut them off, but I needed her to be mobile if we were going to get out of here undetected. Sound carried over water, so I motioned with my hand for her to make her way towards the shore.

Curious fish swam around us, a little startled by our presence. Once they got used to the idea of huge humans moving through their space, though, they swam happily around us, as if we were part of their environment.

Finally, Valentina and I made it to shore. I pulled myself up first so that I could pull Valentina up. It wasn't an unreasonable jump for someone more than 6 feet tall, but Valentina would never be able to make it up by herself quietly. I pulled her into my arms and kissed her.

Then I kissed her again. I pressed my hips against her, showing her that I was erect.

"This isn't the time," she hissed. "Oh my god, they're shooting at each other."

"Nobody's paying attention," I whispered into her ear. "And as long as you can stay quiet, nobody's going to notice what we're doing. Valentina, I just watched someone put a gun to your head. I need to know that you're fine..that we're fine. We'll talk later, when talking won't get us killed."

Instead of responding, she slowly flipped up her skirt. A second later, her panties were in her hand.

"Is that a yes?"

She nodded.

Tree

Allen

I pushed her back against a tree. Skirts were a fabulous invention. If I had my way, Valentina would only wear skirts and dresses from now on. They allowed all kinds of access. I buried a single finger inside of her, stroking her front wall, finding her g-spot. She stifled a moan, her eyes closed, and I licked her neck, tasting the salt from the ocean.

With my other hand, I unzipped my pants. I regretted taking my finger out of her, but I had to do it if I wanted to get my pants off. Then they were around my ankles before I kicked them off and nudged my erection between Valentina's thighs. She was trembling, and I didn't know if it was from lust or the incredible scare that we'd just been through. Probably both.

We both gritted our teeth to stifle the groans that we wanted to let out when I finally entered her. After getting out of the water, I was a little cold; getting inside of her warmed me up nicely. I buried my face in her neck as I braced my arms against the tree behind her.

Her head was tilted back, her chin pointing up. I kept thrusting inside of her, but I wanted to change the angle. I pulled out of her, and when Valentina opened her eyes, I spun her quickly so that her front was against the tree. I parted her legs by kicking them apart and putting my feet inside of hers, then I slid back inside of her warm body.

She was breathing hard and very quietly now, and it turned me on to think that someone could see us any minute. I didn't want anybody else to see Valentina like this, of course, and they'd leave us alone if they knew what we were doing. Still, I had to admit to a certain thrill when I thought of fucking her outside.

Her muscles clenched and quivered around me. I knew that she was close, so I went to pinch her clit. When she cried out, I put one hand over her mouth so that nobody would find us. Her entire body was shaking with the force of her orgasm now, and I wouldn't be able to hold on for much longer.

With a muffled grunt, I spilled my seed inside of her body. I thought of the child that she already had growing inside of her. I wouldn't repeat the same mistakes that I'd made when I had Trouble. Twenty-odd years ago, I'd been consumed by an overwhelming grief that lasted far beyond the year that the DSM 5 allowed for normal grief. I'd be a better father to both of my children, and maybe Valentina would finally let me fill the house with a baker's dozen of kids. Maybe more.

I pulled out of her and let her skirt drop. Her panties were still clutched in her hand; I stole them before she could react and put them in my pocket.

"Souvenir," I whispered.

"Dirty," she whispered back.

I patted her fine ass before putting my wet pants back on.

"You know it."

The gunfire had stopped. I looked around. The boat was dead in the water, and the inflatable raft was getting closer and closer to it. I could see that Sergio and Severin were still in the boat; they probably didn't understand the properties of water resistance. It seemed shortsighted of them not to wear body armor when kidnapping my woman, but they apparently hadn't expected this confrontation any more than I had.

I could make noise now, so I put

my arm around the mother of my child and took her towards the other guards. From our disheveled hair and clothing, they could probably see that we'd fucked in the forest. They didn't say a word, though, and Anthony drove us back to the house on the path that went around the perimeter of the island.

"Don't ever fucking steal my weapon again," he warned. "You're a fucking bastard."

"There's a lady present," I snapped.

"Sorry," he told Valentina. "But he left me without a gun."

"That was foolish," she said in her sweet voice.

"If I hadn't run down there, they would've cast off and been gone before our reinforcements arrived."

"You could have died," Valentina told me. "It was crazy to go down there."

"I'd do a lot more for you and the baby," I said, reaching forward until my hand rested on her baby bump. "I'd do far, far more."

"You expecting a kid?" Anthony cut in, listening to our private conversation. I backed up from Valentina and crossed my arms.

"Yes."

"Congratulations, sir."

"Thank you."

I reached back for Valentina's hand; she squeezed mine as we bumped along the path all the way back to the main house.

Warm

Allen

"You're shivering," I told her.
"Let's get out of our wet clothes and
soak in my Jacuzzi to warm up."

We went upstairs to our
bedroom. I realized that she didn't
have any clothes at the moment,
since her suitcase was in the plane.
She'd just have to wear some of mine
until we could get someone to go
back there and get all of her stuff. I

was way taller than she was, and my shirts were the length of her dresses. For some reason, the idea of Valentina wearing my clothes turned me on.

She was naked then, and I touched her soft, dark skin softly before I went to turn on the tap. I shucked off my clothes, then I climbed inside of the tub. She came in next to me.

I leaned forward to claim her mouth in a passionate kiss, one hand in her hair. The other hand was moving her legs apart so that I could stimulate her clit as we made out.

Our kiss lasted for what seemed like forever. Our tongues danced while she made little noises in the back of her throat that meant that she was close to orgasm. Whenever she started shaking, though, I'd back off. I kept her near the edge of orgasm for long enough for Valentina to finally break the kiss.

She was standing now, the water dripping off of her body. She looked like a goddess, pure, perfect curves everywhere. I leaned forward to suck on her dark nipple. She yelped in front of me before putting her hands in my hair and holding me close.

I slid easily downward to lick the clit that I'd just played with.

"Allen!"

"Valentina," I murmured into her soft lips. "Mmm." I licked her from the bottom to the top, one hand pushing a finger inside of her soft walls that were already dripping honey. I wanted to eat all of it.

Her legs started shaking with

that orgasm that I hadn't let her have, so I swept her legs from under her and caught her in my arms. Before she could even blink, my hand was between her legs. She was writhing in my lap, eyes tightly shut, face contorted in ecstasy as she finally found completion.

I circled her clit again and again; Valentina screamed now, screamed all the sound that we hadn't been able to make while we were near the mangroves. It echoed off of the tile, and I was surrounded by the sound of her passion.

Eventually, she was panting hard. She straddled my lap and kissed me while her hand went to find my cock. Even though we'd had sex not too long ago, going down on her had definitely made me hard again. She stroked up and down expertly, touching just the right spots. I moaned into her mouth.

When I felt a spurt of precome come out, I broke our kiss, then I put my hands on her hips and guided her onto my cock. We both moaned as I slid my erection inside of her.

"I will never let anybody hurt you," I promised her. "I never want to see anybody slap you or point a gun to your head again. You're going to have 3 bodyguards at all times. Maybe 5. No, that's not enough. It's got to be 10."

She giggled. "I'd never be able to go anywhere if I had 10 bodyguards." She stroked my head. "I'll have to negotiate you down. I'll start with one."

"Nice try, babe," I told her,

smiling. "But I'm not going to budge."

"We'll see about that," she said, rocking her hips on me. She tilted her head so that she kissed the side of my neck before biting my ear.

That was it. My hands pulled her even closer to me so that there wasn't any water between us at all. She rode on top of me, splashing water everywhere. I bit her shoulder as I spurted inside of her beautiful body. I could feel her fluttering around me as I thrust and spilled jet after jet of hot seed inside of her.

When I could think again, I opened my eyes. Her face was filled with utter bliss and happiness. A small smile was lurking around the corner of her mouth.

"We need to talk about the baby."

The smile disappeared. "We do."

I put my hand on her stomach. "Watching you and the baby being kidnapped made me realize how much you both mean to me. I would die before aborting the child or encouraging you to have an abortion."

"You mean that?" she asked me, her eyes a little glassy.

"I do," I told her before I captured her mouth in a kiss.

I was the one to break the kiss this time.

"I've got something for you. Stay here."

I got out of the tub and dried off quickly in a towel before putting it back on the rack. I went to the nightstand drawer and pulled out a small blue box.

Totally naked and not caring, I

walked back into the bathroom. I brought the box into the tub, splashing a little.

"I was going to do this at a dinner that I had cooked for you. I was going to bring in a band to serenade you. There were going to be candles, roses, and chicken parmigiana."

She was staring at the box.

"Is that—?"

I flipped it open so that she could see what was inside. I'd asked Tiffany's for the largest rock that a woman could comfortably wear, and it had thrown a million rainbows when they'd showed it to me in the store. It wasn't pre-made; I'd bought it custom made, because Tiffany's didn't just hand out expensive, large diamonds to casual browsers.

Her hands were over her mouth now, and her chest was heaving while she gulped in air. I had to admit that I liked the way that her breasts were moving.

"Valentina, would you do me the honor of becoming my wife?"

"How long have you had that

box?"

"A long time," I told her. "I was going to wait for the perfect night, but today taught me that life is for living right now. I needed to be sure that I could handle a wife and kid again, and after today, I'm absolutely sure that you're the only one for me. This is right, and I feel it in my bones."

"What about Adeline?"

"I will always love Adeline. But she is part of my past, and you are part of my future, if you want to be."

She stared at the rock in my

hand. "Can I get a smaller size? I feel like lifting that thing will be like lifting weights."

I smiled. "Anything you want, babe. Is that a yes?"

She nodded, and I pulled the ring out of the box to slide it onto her ring finger. Both of us looked at it shining in the light of the bathroom and throwing little rainbows everywhere around us. One of them was on her face; I kissed it before trailing down to her neck and the tops of her breasts. I bit one softly, and she gasped next to my ear.

"You've made me very happy," I said, lifting my head so that I could gaze into her beautiful dark eyes.

"I will be glad to be your wife."

Her arms came around me, and her whole body was wrapped around mine as we kissed to seal the deal.

Epilogue

Allen

I adjusted my bow-tie in the mirror when my caterer, a blond lady named Deanne, knocked on the door. Her hair was a total mess, and she was hyperventilating. My instincts kicked in.

"What's wrong?"

She tried to catch her breath before saying, "There's no more pinot noir, sir! What will we do?"

"There's plenty of other wine, though, isn't there?"

"Not the right kind! We've accidentally served everything that we had beforehand, since people kept requesting it."

Deanne looked close to tears, so I told her, "I don't care about the wine. Go send someone to the liquor store and bill me for it."

She nodded, then she ran out of the room to get more stock.

So flighty.

Valentina wasn't like Deanne.

She was solid of heart, and I knew that with her by my side, I could conquer the world. I could even think about retiring. Now that I had someone to be with, I definitely had a reason to be home more often. I thought about the life growing inside of her, a son or daughter that I'd raise with Valentina by my side. My grandson could be playmates with my new child.

Trouble came into the room then.

"Dad, it's time." We'd spent a lot of time together, and Valentina and

Laila had gone to pre-natal classes, dragging me along every single time. Trouble somehow managed to get out of it, only coming to a few. I knew more about Lamaze techniques than I ever wanted to. I had also learned how to put a diaper on a baby and test milk in a bottle to see if it was too hot. All of these things were new to me, so I'd paid attention. Valentina had laughed when she saw me taking a video on my phone of the instructor putting a diaper on a doll, but I had a fierce desire to do everything right this time.

Trouble was my best man, of course. My ring bearer was a distant cousin's son who was the right age. He had the satin pillow in his hand, which had rings that would bind us together forever.

We walked into the small chapel. I had plenty of business associates, of course, and I'd planned a huge wedding. I wanted to shout to the world that I was marrying the most wonderful woman imaginable.

Her side was full, too. She had so

many friends and family members who were happy to be part of her special day. I'd gone through some tough questions when I'd gone over to her family's home in Indianapolis for dinner, but they'd eventually warmed up to me, even though they teased me sometimes.

I stood next to the judge. Neither of us was particularly religious, so we could have had a simple ceremony in a courthouse. But I wanted to throw a lavish wedding and invite distant relations, so here we were.

The quartet that I had hired started to play the wedding march, and all eyes were on the back of the chapel. Valentina was holding a bouquet of pink orchids, her favorite flowers. We'd had a whirlwind romance, but I knew that we would go the distance.

Finally, her dad was stopping near me. She climbed the steps as he turned away to sit in the front row.

I held her hands and stared into her eyes, which were tearing up. I barely heard the judge saying the words, slowly repeating my vows as he fed them to me. It was her turn.

Then the judge said that we were married. I kissed her hard, leaning her back, cheers coming from our audience. The dress had been cut to carefully conceal her baby bump. The baby would be born less than nine months after the wedding. I didn't feel like we had anything to be ashamed of, but Valentina wanted to keep her pregnancy a secret for now for the sake of her career. She wasn't that far along, and I'd caved. When it came to the children, her vote would always count more than mine.

The two of us held hands as everyone threw rice at us while we walked out to the limo. It said "Just Married" on the back. It would take us to the country club where we were holding our reception.

* * *

Three hours later, I was pleasantly buzzed. Dinner had been fabulous and simple. Some of her distant relations were vegetarians, so we had pasta, salmon, and beef on our RSVP. We had been asked to kiss so many times that my lips felt swollen, but I couldn't stop a shit-eating grin from staying there. Valentina was my life now.

When some of my older relations started to shake my hand before they went home, I whispered in Valentina's ear, "Let's go home."

She squeezed my hand. She knew what was waiting for her. We told the DJ to make the announcement that the two of us were leaving, and somebody found a basket of rice somewhere and threw it all over us. Valentina had changed into a simple dress for the reception with lower heels so that she could dance. No matter what size heels she wore, she'd always be shorter than me, unless she wore actual stilts.

I loved dancing with her, but I was also impatient to get her out of her dress. It was stunning, sure, but I knew what she looked like out of it.

When we were done saying goodbye, the two of us walked out to my car. I'd brought it to the country club earlier. Trouble had driven me to the chapel. We got into the car.

Valentina yawned. "Phew, what a day."

"It's not over yet." I put my hand on her thigh.

Her eyes drifted shut. "I've been up since 5 with preparations for the wedding. You have no idea how much time we had to spend on hair and makeup for my bridesmaids."

"Sleep now," I told her. "Believe me, you're going to need it."

She tilted her head so that it

rested on her seatbelt. I drove us home. So what if I broke the speed limit?

When we got home, I got out of the car and raced around so that I could open her door. When I opened it, she opened her eyes.

"Are we home?"

"Yeah, babe." I leaned over her body. She smelled good, just like those pink orchids that she'd been carrying earlier. I unbuckled her, then I picked her up in my arms.

"Allen!" she squealed, throwing

her arms around my neck to hold onto me. "Put me down! I'm too heavy for this!"

"Babe, you're a foot shorter than me. Trust me, I can handle this."

I brought my bride to the threshold and carried her over it. I even ran up the stairs with her in my arms. Her eyes were looking into mine, and it was a miracle that we didn't wipe out on the stairs.

Then we were finally in my bedroom. Trouble and Laila had found their own place, of course, so we had the house to ourselves. They weren't too far away, though, so we would always be able to gather for family dinners. I put her down on her feet.

"I like the dress," I told her. "I just like you better out of it."

I ripped it off of her body.

"Oh my goodness!" she shouted. "Do you have any idea what it cost?"

"Babe, I can buy you ten more and never notice anything." I kissed her exposed collarbone. "I like your lingerie."

Underneath her modest reception dress, she was wearing some kind of corset and garter set. I had to say that I approved of the bridal white. It looked very, very good on her.

I spun her and bent her over the edge of my bed. I found the million little hooks down the back of the corset, and I figured out how to unhook all of them. Then it was simple to unhook her garters and roll her stockings down her legs. The stockings were soft, but her skin was softer.

I kissed my way up from her ankle to the backs of her knees and then to the inner parts of her thighs, tasting the salt of her sweat on her skin. Then I went for her core, and she moaned in front of me as I gave her pleasure, making sure to rub her clit against the edge of the bed. It was sexy, because I was fully clothed while she was totally naked.

We stayed there for a while, me pushing my tongue in and against her, her rocking back onto my mouth. When I felt myself leaking precome, I knew that I had to consummate my marriage.

I stood up and took off my tuxedo, throwing it in the corner. I owned it, of course, and I could abuse it as much as I liked. My boxers were on the floor only moments later, and then I was guiding myself inside of my lovely bride.

I noticed that her fists were clenched, holding the bedspread tightly as I thrust into her with a slow, rolling rhythm. Especially the first time that we made love as husband and wife, I wanted to make sweet love to her. We'd had plenty of the quick and dirty kind of rendezvous. I wanted her to know that my primary thought from now on was to ensure her pleasure — to make sure that she was my highest priority. Always.

That's why my hand snuck around her front to rub her clit until she orgasmed once. Twice. Three times. And then so many times that I couldn't count, only grit my teeth and hold the base of my cock so that I wouldn't come.

She felt like heaven around me, warm and wet. I could watch her breathing hard as I picked up the pace again.

This time, I was aching to spill myself into her. I pulled apart her thighs so that they were a little wider as I thrust into her so hard that her feet left the floor and the headboard banged against the wall. The headboard began to pound out the rhythm of our lovemaking, an accompaniment to the consummation of my marriage.

"You're mine," I told her. "Always."

"Always," she agreed.

Then my eyes rolled back in my head as I emptied everything inside of her — all of me. I'd give her everything I could.

When it was done, I pulled out of her body, which was still quivering. I got on the bed with her and held her in the circle of my arms. I bit her shoulder and then her ear. I planted a necklace of kisses on her neck, and I felt her breathing quicken until she was panting her way through a small orgasm again, a small orgasm which I helped along by putting my hand between her thighs.

"Satisfied, Mrs. McKane?"

"Exhausted, Mr. McKane."

I kept a hand on the front edge of her curvy thigh while my front was pressed to her soft back.

"Good night," she told me.

"Goodnight," I told her for the first night of what would be a lifetime of nights spent together.

Epilogue Two

SEVERAL MONTHS LATER

The nurse came back into the room and put my newborn baby girl in my arms. Her little eyes were closed, her lashes touching her cheeks. She had a little bit of fuzzy hair. Her little rosebud mouth was in a big pout, even when she was asleep, and I knew that she'd be an adorable tyrant and get away with it.

Her tiny little hands with teensy

little fingers and nails were kept inside of the blanket. I unwrapped her a little so that she'd have a little more freedom of movement. I touched her little foot, which was smaller than my thumb, so that I could tickle it. She kicked me in her sleep and fussed a little.

I smiled. I was going to have fun raising my little girl, baby Willa.

Her mother opened her eyes, even though she was exhausted and sweaty from the hours she'd spent in labor.

"Let me hold my baby."

I brought little Willa to her mother. Valentina reached for her, and when she put Willa's face onto her shoulder, the baby nuzzled her a little bit.

I heard footsteps as someone came through the door.

"Hi, Dad."

"Trouble," I said, hugging him. "Meet your little sister."

Laila was right behind Trouble, holding a baby carrier that held my grandson, baby Zachary. He was only a few months old, and like his aunt, he was fast asleep. He was bundled up in a jacket and hat since it was pretty chilly today.

I looked around the room. My whole family was here; their love was worth more than the billions that I'd amassed. I'd been reborn, and I had to admit that it'd taken work, but I was finally the man I was meant to be.

THE END

This is a work of fiction intended for mature audiences only. Names, characters, places, and incident either are the product of the author's imagination or are used fictitiously. Any resemblance to events, locales, business establishments, or actual persons, living or dead, events, or locales is purely coincidental.

All sexual activities depicted occur between consenting characters 18 years or older and who are not blood related.